Torn Pages

Also by Sally Grindley

Broken Glass
Spilled Water
Saving Finnegan
Hurricane Wills
Feather Wars

Torn Pages

Sally Grindley

BLOOMSBURY

LONDON BERLIN NEW YORK

Bloomsbury Publishing, London, Berlin and New York

First published in Great Britain in 2009 by Bloomsbury Publishing Plc
36 Soho Square, London, W1D 3QY

A CIP catalogue record of this book is available from the British Library

ISBN 978 0 7475 9505 2

The paper this book is printed on is certified independently in accordance with the rules
of the FSC. It is ancient-forest friendly. The printer holds chain of custody

FSC
Mixed Sources
Product group from well-managed
forests and other controlled sources
www.fsc.org
Cert no. SGS - COC - 2061
www.fsc.org
© 1996 Forest Stewardship Council

Typeset by Hewer Text UK Ltd, Edinburgh
Printed in Great Britain by Clays Ltd, St Ives plc

1 3 5 7 9 10 8 6 4 2

www.bloomsbury.com/childrens
www.sallygrindley.co.uk

For my mum, still full of beans at 80

Chapter 1

Do you remember, Lydia, when the mighty storm came, how lightning split the sky in two and thunder broke the night like a charge of elephants? You stood twitching by my bed, hoping to be invited in, when an orange dropped with a crash on to the roof from the tree outside the window. You leapt in the air like somebody had put a scorpion down your knickers, and landed right on top of me — OOMPH! You took my breath away with your bony elbows and nearly made your brother arrive early into the world. Do you remember how you giggled when I asked you how come you were suddenly so afraid of oranges? 'It's not the oranges,' you protested, and I teased you, saying you must be the only little girl in the whole of Africa to leap out of her skin because of an orange.

We lay there and waited for the storm to wear it-self out. You sniggered when Baba turned warthog and grunted and snuffled as though searching for roots. You said we should put him out in the yard. He woke just as you said it, told you not to be a cheeky monkey, then went straight back to his grunting, only worse. The baby started kicking then. Perhaps he too was frightened by the storm, or the orange, or your father's snoring. You put your hand on the dome of my belly and felt a tiny foot slide across under the skin. You asked if I would let you help look after the baby when he was born. You said it would be good practice because you wanted to be a nurse when you grew up. I said what a big ambition that was for a little five-year-old. I said you could be the baby's second mummy and what a lucky baby he would be.

As the storm began to move away, I told you stor-ies about the trickster rabbit and the lion king, un-til your eyes became so heavy that, even if all the oranges in the world had fallen on to the roof, they could not have kept you from sleeping.

There's something about a storm in the middle of the night that gathers a family close. It's as if nothing else exists outside that huddle of love in a blacked-out room which, try as it might, the storm cannot overwhelm. Remember that closeness, Lydia, my child, and try to carry it with you through every dawning day.

Lydia shifted in the bed and dislodged her brother's knee from her hip. Outside, the storm had blown itself hollow and all that was left was the drip, drip, drip of raindrops on the upturned tin bath. On the other side of her brother, Kesi, their sister, was restless in her sleep, little wisps of anxiety escaping with each breath. Lydia leant across and stroked her hair, such thick, coarse hair, until she saw her lips relax into a flicker of a smile. At what point in their dreams had Kesi changed places with her brother, for she had begun the night as usual, tucked in the middle, safe from any evil spirits that might lurk under the bed?

Lydia wondered when it would be morning. The sky was still deep black through the window beyond the candle flame, but how much of that was just lingering clouds? She didn't know how long she had been asleep before the storm had woken her. It wasn't a mighty storm like the one her mother had described. Kesi and Joe had slept right through it. She hadn't been able to go back to sleep herself and had lit the candle so that she could read her mother's book. She wasn't sure she wanted it to be morning. The night provided some respite from the drudgery of the day, from the problems that heaped themselves upon her however much she tried her hardest to avoid them. Sometimes it was all too much.

You will never be alone, Lydia, she read. I will always be there for you. Find your strength from me. Be that person we talked about who can climb the tallest tree and touch the moon.

'I can't even see the moon, Mama,' she sighed.

She put the book carefully on the floor, blew out the candle, lay back down and closed her eyes.

Chapter 2

'She's wet the bed again, Liddy,' a voice hissed in her ear.

'It's not my fault,' another voice wailed.

Lydia dragged herself from her sleep. A soft, warm arm wrapped itself round her neck as she tried to sit up.

'Don't be cross, Liddy. I didn't mean to do it.'

'I hate waking up soaked in your wee.'

'I'm soaked too.' Kesi's hair frizzled across Lydia's face as she gripped her tighter.

'Let me breathe, will you?' Lydia muttered.

Kesi dropped her arm but nuzzled her head into her sister's chest. Lydia pushed her gently away and struggled to her feet.

'It's my fault,' she said. 'I should have woken you up to go, but you were sleeping so deeply.'

'I'm going to sleep on the ground tonight,' growled Joe.

'You'll get covered in creepy crawlies,' squealed Kesi.

'Better than wee,' Joe replied.

'We'll get you washed before Grandma finds out,' said Lydia.

'You won't tell her, will you?' Kesi aimed at Joe.

Joe didn't answer.

'He's going to tell her, Liddy, and then she'll make you send me away,' said Kesi.

'Don't tease her, Joe,' said Lydia.

'What does she take me for? Course I won't tell.' He stamped on a beetle that ran across the floor, picked up a water jug and stomped out of the rondavel.

Joe must be really fed up, thought Lydia. *It's unlike him to sound quite so grumpy.*

'Come on then, Kes,' she sighed. 'Let's get the bed changed.'

'I didn't used to wet it,' Kesi said quietly.

'No, I know you didn't. And soon you won't do it again.' Lydia pulled away the damp sheet. 'It's because you're upset about Mama.'

'I expect I wouldn't do it if she came back,' suggested Kesi.

'She's not coming back, you know that, Kes.'

Kesi sat at the table and watched as her sister rolled up the sheet and put it by the door of their home. 'I'm hungry,' she whined. 'When are we going to eat?'

What are we going to eat? Lydia asked herself.

She gazed across the garden. It was a mass of tangled stems and leaves, flattened by the pummelling of the rain in the night. A thin cloud of steam rose up as the morning sun sucked the moisture from the plants and began to dry them. Lydia wondered, if she stared hard enough, whether she might see the stems spring up-right again, all in one go. They were weeds, most of them, and seemed to have devoured the rows of vegetables she had planted so painstakingly while her mother watched, too ill to help. She knew she should set about them to allow the vegetables a chance to breathe, but there never seemed to be the time, and the ground was so hard that it was impossible to pull the weeds out without breaking off their heads. When that happened, it wasn't long before they started pushing up again, only twice as big and twice as strong and twice as fast. The vegetables didn't grow like that. Once Lydia had discovered the feathery top of a carrot and tried to pull it out. The top had come away, leaving the carrot behind. She had dug at the ground until she had freed the carrot, only to find that it was as small as her thumb and eaten away on one side.

The garden is your larder, Lydia. Look after it well and it will look after you.

The weeds had taken over very fast. Lydia had intended to dig them out every day, but when her mother became so ill that she couldn't get out of bed, there had been too many other things to do and her mother needed her there beside her.

When I no longer have the strength to speak, Lydia, stay with me. Take Joe and Kesi to your grandmother, then stay with me. Hold my hand and read to me from my book. Read to me about the good times we've had together and help me to smile. It's my book to you to help you when I am gone. And it's my book to me, to remind me of who I was.

For the first few weeks after their mother died, Lydia had felt too numb to do very much. There was the funeral to get through. Kesi clung to her constantly, while Joe hid himself in bushes close to their homestead for hours on end and wouldn't come out, no matter how hard she begged. It was just three days after Joe had finally abandoned his hideout that their wheelbarrow disappeared, together with a coat their father used to wrap round himself to keep warm when his illness made him shiver and which their mother had kept, saying that one day it would serve Joe well. They had used the wheelbarrow to fetch firewood, to bring back jugs of water and to carry rubbish to the tip. Joe was so angry when he discovered it had gone that he marched from homestead to homestead in the village, demanding to know if anyone had seen anything. A few of the villagers hurled abuse at him, but it didn't stop him. He was determined to find the culprit. It was only when he saw the wheelbarrow piled high with rubble, sitting outside the house of a local builder, that he gave up. Two dogs were tied up close by and they snarled menacingly at him the minute he stepped towards them.

'It's so unfair,' he protested to Lydia when he got back home. 'It's our barrow and we can't do anything about it.'

'We'll have to forget about it, Joe,' she said. 'There's no good going on about it. And Mama warned us what it would be like.'

You'll have to be strong, Lydia. There are those, like your father's mother, who blame me for what's happened, and because you are my children they think you carry the same curse through your veins. There are those who think we brought this upon ourselves, and those who think we'll bring them down with us just by breathing the same air. Choose your friends carefully, my child. Be sure their heads are wise and their hearts warm.

Joe reappeared through the hedge at the bottom of the garden, the jug of water balanced on his head. He had washed himself while he was away and was soaking wet. He trekked through to the kitchen and tipped the water into a plastic bowl on the small table.

'Mr Hlabisa was there,' he said, dropping the empty jug on the ground. 'He told me I had to wait till everybody else had gone first. He told me we should go somewhere else because nobody wanted us polluting their water. Mr Namile told him to leave me alone and that he was the one who was polluted. I thought they were going to have a fight.'

'Poor Joe,' said Lydia, trying to put her arm round him. At thirteen, she felt that she should be able to cope with most things, but her brother was only just nine and she was desperate to protect him as much as possible.

He shrugged out of the way. 'I don't care,' he growled. He went outside and flopped down on the ground with his back against the rondavel. He picked up a long stick and began to strip off the bark.

'When are we going to eat?' Kesi demanded again.

'When I've washed you,' said Lydia. She lifted her sister on to the table and noticed how thin she was becoming. She took a piece of rag and wiped her down.

'Is Joe still cross with me, Liddy?' Kesi asked.

'No,' Lydia replied. 'He's cross with other people.'

'Are other people being not nice to him?'

Lydia lifted her down. 'I think I saw a mango on the tree,' she said. 'Run and see if you can reach it.'

Kesi skipped out of the kitchen. Lydia washed herself, collected the tin bath from outside and tipped the water from the plastic bowl into it. She put the soiled sheet into the bath and began to pummel it. She could have done with some more water, but she didn't want to ask Joe to go back, and didn't want to risk being absent when their grandmother turned up. She kneaded the sheet a few more times and was about to wring it out when there was a loud scream. Lydia turned to see Joe sprinting across the garden. She dropped the sheet and ran outside. Over by the mango tree, Kesi was holding her hands between her legs and crying her eyes out. Joe was squatting next to her, trying to calm her down.

'Hurts,' Kesi sobbed. 'The bee stung me.'

'Let me look, Kes,' Joe said. 'I might be able to get the sting out.'

'No,' Kesi wailed. 'I don't want it to hurt more.'

'We need to get the sting out if it's a bee, Kes,' said Lydia. 'I promise we won't hurt you.'

'It was in the mango,' Kesi sobbed again.

She slowly pulled her hand from between her legs and was about to hold it out to Lydia when a voice demanded, 'What's all the fuss about this time?'

Lydia, Joe and Kesi looked up to see their grandmother striding towards them.

'Kesi's been stung by a bee,' Joe informed her.

'I expect she asked for it,' Grandma Motsie sniffed. 'Let me see.'

Kesi hid her hand again. 'Don't want you to see it,' she howled.

'Don't be so silly,' snapped her grandmother. 'We can't help you if you're going to be silly.'

'Hold your hand out, Kes,' said Lydia softly.

'It's not as if I'm going to touch you,' said the old woman with distaste.

Kesi slowly held out her hand. There was a livid red swelling in the middle of her palm.

Grandma Motsie screwed up her nose. 'You'd better see if you can get the sting out for her,' she said.

Joe put his arm round Kesi's shoulders while Lydia knelt down and took her by the wrist. 'I'll be as gentle as I can,' she said. 'It'll feel better with the sting gone.'

'Are you going to suck it out?' asked Joe.

'No she's not,' their grandmother said sharply. 'She can squeeze it out with a piece of rag.'

'I don't want you to squeeze it out, Liddy,' snivelled Kesi. 'You'll make it hurt more.'

'You squeeze my hand while Liddy squeezes yours,' said Joe. 'Then if Liddy hurts you, you can hurt me.'

Kesi giggled slightly and had a practice squeeze of Joe's hand.

'Ow, ow, ow!' he cried.

Kesi giggled again. As she did, Lydia pinched round the sides of the sting and was relieved to see it squirt out. 'All done,' she said.

'Such a fuss about nothing,' said Grandma Motsie. 'Now, I've brought you some yams. It's not much, but

I wasn't expecting to have three extra mouths to feed at my time of life.'

'Thank you, Grandma,' said Lydia. 'We're very grateful to you.'

'I should think so. Now, fetch some water, Joe, so that we can get them washed, then off to the fields with you. I've heard they're short of labour, so it's a chance for you to earn some money for your family.'

Joe shot Lydia a look of alarm.

'It's a schoolday, Grandma,' she said. 'Joe's got school to go to.'

'Joe won't be going to school any more, and neither will your sister. We can't afford it, especially if we have to start wasting money on medicines.'

Lydia glared at her grandmother. 'But Mama made me promise that I would keep them in school.'

'And how do you think the school fees are to be paid?'

'With the money she saved.'

'Your mother was a fool if she thought that money would last five minutes. It hasn't lasted five seconds.'

I have been careful, Lydia. It's been so hard, hasn't it, since your father died? While I can still earn, I am put—

ting money away so that you and Joe and Kesi can carry on going to school when I have gone. It means that we have less to live on now and go hungry sometimes, but it means too that I am saving money to help secure your future. You must go to school, all of you. It's the only way to give yourselves the chance of something better.

'There must be some money left,' Lydia protested.

'Are you accusing me of stealing now?' the old woman rounded on her. 'If anybody should be accused it's your mother for taking a good son from his own mother and poisoning him.'

Lydia flinched. She already knew that Grandma Motsie blamed her mother for her father's death. She had heard it so many times before. She had heard the sharp tongue lashing, from the moment it became clear that her father would not survive the illness that changed him from the strong, devil-may-care Baba she loved into a wizened, bedridden old man. She had seen her grandmother gossiping in the village, turning some of the older villagers against her mother with tales of witchcraft and sorcery. Even when they had first moved back from the town and her father had seemed to be well, Lydia had overheard her grandmother telling him that he had married the wrong woman, could have done better for himself, shouldn't trust her, would be let down by her. To his credit, her father had laughed it off, telling his mother that she was jealous and that no wife of his would ever be good enough as far as she was concerned. Lydia wanted to defend her mother, but she didn't want to aggravate her grand-mother. She was the only adult left in their lives and Lydia was afraid of what might happen if she abandoned them.

'I just meant that I thought it would last a lot longer,' Lydia said meekly.

'Well, I haven't been spending it on myself,' said the old woman, which was just what Lydia thought she might have been doing when she noticed her new shoes.

'Is there really no money left?' she couldn't help but ask again. 'Mama said if we don't go to school, we'll never get a good job. Then we'll always have to rely on you.'

'Hmmm, I'll be in my grave by then, so you'll have to sort yourselves out. Anyway, not going to school never did me any harm.'

'You sent Baba to school,' Lydia dared to continue.

'He was worth it,' snapped her grandmother. 'Now that's enough of your arguing. The money's gone, there'll be no more school, and you can all start doing some work so that I don't have to spend my old age running around after you.'

Lydia stared at her in astonishment. Kesi threw her arms round Lydia's legs and buried her head, while Joe grabbed the water jug and ran out of the garden. The old woman picked up the bag of yams and headed for the rondavel.

'We'll manage on our own then,' Lydia muttered under her breath. She detached Kesi and hurried after her grandmother. She was too late, though, to stop her from discovering the wet sheet in the tin bath.

'Another wet bed?' her grandmother asked with distaste.

'The sheet just needed washing, that's all,' Lydia said quickly.

'And you think this nose of mine can't pick up the smell of urine after all these years? You think I don't know what the dark patch on the mattress is? That child needs a good smack – that will soon stop it.'

'She misses Mama.'

The old woman dropped the bag of yams to the floor. 'Your mother's been dead four months. It's time that child got used to it – she's five years old, she's not a baby any more. You'll have to deal with the yams yourself. I'm not touching that sheet, and if you had any sense you'd make her clean it herself.' She pushed past Lydia and hurried away.

Lydia sat down on the bed and put her head in her hands.

Try to be understanding with your grandmother, Lydia. She is still hurting from losing her son, your father. She cannot bear to think he might have done anything wrong. In three short years, she lost the two people she loved most in her life. When your grandfather, her husband, was killed by a truck, it was your father who gave her the will to carry on. When he died too, she turned her grief into bitterness. She had to have some— body to blame and so she blames me. I can cope with that, Lydia, and so must you. When I am gone, it will be your grandmother who takes care of you and Joe and little Kesi. I am sure she will do her best to keep you safe and happy.

Kesi sat down on the bed next to her. 'Why is Grand- ma so horrible to us?' she asked. 'Why doesn't she like me?'

'She's old, Kes. She doesn't want the bother of having to look after us. And she's sad because Baba died.'

'You won't smack me, will you, Liddy?' Kesi pressed her nose against Lydia's arm. 'I'll wash the sheet if you want me to.'

'Of course I won't smack you,' sighed Lydia, 'and neither will Grandma. I won't let her.'

They sat quietly for a moment, then Kesi murmured, 'I don't mind not going to school.'

'You have to go to school, even if it means I have to work twenty-four hours a day to find the money,' Lydia said firmly.

'Some of the boys and girls aren't very nice to me any more.'

'What do you mean they're not nice to you?'

'They call me nasty names and say if anybody touches me they'll die.'

'You know that's not true.' Lydia pulled her sister closer. 'See, I'm touching you and I'm fine.'

'They say I've got witch's blood in me and that soon I'll shrivel up and turn into a toad.'

'Why didn't you tell me, Kes? If anyone's got witch's blood in them it's the ones who say things like that, and they deserve to turn into toads themselves. You've got the same blood as me and Joe, and just because we're orphans doesn't mean that we have to listen to them saying things like that.'

19

'They say Mama filled me up with poison because she didn't like me.'

'Who's saying those things, Kes? Tell me who.' Lydia was horrified at what she was hearing.

'Some of the boys and girls are nice to me, then the nasty ones say things to make them not nice to me.'

'Poor Kes. You just wait till I talk to Mrs Buthelezi, she'll soon stop all that.'

'She makes me sit in the corner with Themba and Patrick,' Kesi whimpered.

Lydia could feel her anger mounting. 'Why? Why does she do that? You haven't been naughty, have you?'

'She says it's better for us because some people don't want their children to sit next to us.'

Lydia stood up sharply. 'There's nothing wrong with you, Kes, nothing. I'm going to go and see Mrs Buthelezi and tell her so, and I'm going to make sure those boys and girls say sorry to you.'

The hardest thing is knowing that I might have spread this terrible disease to little Kesi. If I think of that, I cry an ocean of tears. You and Joe are so healthy because you come from the time when your father gave all his love to me. What changed to make him seek out somebody else I don't understand, but his faithlessness sent him to an early grave, poisoned me and sowed a web of doubt about Kesi's future. I believe with all my heart that she is well, but how can I know what lies just round the corner? I'm scared to have her tested because of what the test might show. Watch over her like a guardian angel, Lydia, and if you see the sickness come, if she wakes with a fever and loses the sparkle of childhood, fetch a doctor to her quickly, no matter how much it costs.

Chapter 3

When Joe came back, he banged the water jug down on the table, then slumped back down on the ground outside the door and grabbed the stick he had been stripping. Lydia had hung out the sheet and moved the mattress into the sun to dry. She stopped sweeping the yard and came and stood next to him.

Neither of them spoke for a moment, until she said, 'Has everything been all right for you at school?'

He looked at her suspiciously. 'Yeah. Why?'

'They've stuck Kesi in a corner and said nobody's to touch her.'

Joe slammed his elbow against the wall of the rondavel. 'I can look after myself,' he growled. 'And I don't care what Grandma says, I'm going to keep going to school.'

'We don't have any money to pay the fees, Joe.'

'I bet Grandma used it all for herself. How can she do that? It was our money. Mama left it for us.' He kicked at the ground, sending clouds of dust into the air. 'I'm going to school. I've just got into the football team. They can't make me stay away.'

Lydia stared at him anxiously. 'We don't know that Grandma used it for herself. Perhaps Mama left less with her than we thought.'

I have been careful, Lydia.

'Will you stay here with Kesi, just while I go and talk to Mrs Buthelezi?' she asked.

Joe pushed out his lip and started picking at his fingernails. 'I've heard some of the kids talking about Kes,' he said quietly. 'I hit one of them, so they don't do it in front of me any more.'

'You should have told me, Joe,' Lydia cried. 'I need to know these things.'

'I didn't know they were doing it to her face,' he retorted. 'Anyway, they're wrong, aren't they? Kes is all right, isn't she?'

'Of course she's all right,' Lydia said firmly. 'She's upset though. She doesn't understand why Grandma and some of the children at school are horrible to her.'

'Grandma's horrible to all of us. I wish she'd just go away and leave us alone.'

Joe stood up and went into the rondavel, where Kesi was playing with a doll.

'Will you wash the yams while I'm gone, please, Joe?' Lydia called after him.

'As long as I can go to school when you get back,' Joe grunted. 'What are we supposed to eat for breakfast?'

'See if you can find something in the garden,' Lydia said quickly, and darted away before she had to listen to any complaints.

She hurried along the path towards the village school, working out in her mind what she was going to say to the teacher and wondering how she would feel when she went through the entrance. She hadn't been inside the school since before their mother died. There hadn't been the time, firstly while she was nursing her, and now that she was having to look after Joe and Kesi. She longed to go back. She missed her friends and being part of the daily school routine. She missed her lessons in English and drama. She was good at drama, her teacher had told her. She had the ability to lose herself in whatever character she was playing and to feel what the character would be feeling.

You made me cry, Lydia, do you know that? You were only ten and you stood up on those rickety boards and turned into a princess in front of my very eyes. When I looked round at your father, I saw that he too was wiping away a tear. Where did it come from, that talent for wrapping yourself up in somebody else's identity and presenting it as your own? Was it from your grandfather, my father, who could tell a joke and make us believe that it was the truth, until he fell about laughing and we realised we had been taken in? He laughed so hard, a great bellow of a laugh that shook the tin roof on our house and set us off as well. Was it from him, or does it come from somewhere further back, from my great-grandparents, who may have had to become someone else just to survive? You may have to become someone else to survive, Lydia. You're a dreamer, and dreamers can fashion roads to Eden, but life has thrown you a challenge that will mean you have to face reality with your eyes wide open. Fix your dreams in the quiet of your mind and never let them go, but be awake to the demands each day will make on you. Joe and Kesi will need your strength and guidance. They will need you to be there for them.

Am I dreaming, Lydia wondered, *by wanting to be back at school? Or am I being realistic, because it's only by going to school that I can better myself?*

She growled and shook her head vigorously. 'Of course I'm dreaming,' she muttered. 'I can't go back to school even if I want to, so I'm not being realistic.'

She walked faster, staring straight ahead of her and trying to think only of what she would say to Mrs Buthelezi. It wasn't until a stone skidded across the ground in front of her that her gaze was diverted. A man she had never seen before was leaning against a tree at the side of the road, grinning at her. He was tall and muscular, and quite good-looking for someone who was a fair bit older than herself.

'Where's the pretty miss going and in such a hurry?' he asked.

Lydia quickly turned her attention away from him and carried on walking.

'Now, I think that's a bit rude not to answer when I'm paying you a nice compliment.'

Lydia walked faster, hoping he wouldn't follow.

'Well, Little Miss Snooty, I guess you're not so pretty then,' he called after her. 'Rather plain and scrawny, actually.'

Under his intense scrutiny, Lydia became so self-conscious that she nearly lost her footing on the uneven surface. She was grateful when she reached a corner and turned to take herself out of his sight. Why he had targeted her she didn't know, but she didn't like it and she prayed that he would be gone when she made her way back home again.

At last Lydia saw the schoolhouse ahead. She hurried towards it, drawn not just by the purpose of her visit, but by the desire for it to welcome her back into its familiar arms. She could hear the school song as she drew closer, and imagined the rows of village children belting it out as they did every morning before classes began. The words played on her lips, she knew them so well. When she reached the steps at the front, she could see through the windows. One of her friends, Sophie, was framed by the window to the right. It had been a while since Lydia had seen her. She waved to attract her attention, but Sophie didn't notice her. Several of the other children saw her and whispered amongst themselves. Lydia drew back and made her way to the entrance, just as the singing stopped and everyone piled out of the main hall into the two classrooms. Mrs Buthelezi shepherded a group of infant boys and girls and smiled at Lydia as she went by. Lydia caught her arm.

'Can I speak with you, please?' she said. 'About Kesi.'

'Is Kesi unwell?' the teacher asked, gazing searchingly at Lydia. 'She's looking thinner.'

'She's fine,' Lydia said, 'but she's upset about being put in the corner.'

Mrs Buthelezi shooed her class into their room before turning back to Lydia. 'Kesi's not the only one there,' she said. 'I've had to separate two other children like her because some of the parents insist on it. In fact, they've asked for us to remove all of them from the school, but we have refused.'

'What do you mean "like her"?' Lydia asked hotly. 'There's nothing wrong with her.'

'No, I'm sure you're right, Lydia, of course you are. But some people have already made up their minds. Now that Kesi is becoming so thin, they'll believe they're right.'

'She's thin because we don't have enough to eat and because she's pining for our mother and because some of the children are being horrible to her.'

'I understand, I do understand,' Mrs Buthelezi said soothingly. 'But I have a job to do and my concern is for all my pupils, not just one or two.'

'My concern is for Kesi,' Lydia countered. 'I promised Mama I would take care of her.'

'Believe me, we are doing our best,' said the teacher, 'but these are difficult circumstances. And now I must attend to my class.'

She turned to go, but stopped when Lydia said, 'Kesi won't be coming back. My grandmother says we have no more money to pay the school fees. Joe's just got into the football team and he's really upset.'

Mrs Buthelezi put her hand on Lydia's shoulder. 'You poor child,' she said. 'As if it weren't enough that you've lost both your parents. Your grandmother must make an appointment to see the Head. I believe that as orphans you may be allowed to attend for free.'

Lydia was surprised and delighted. 'Thank you, Mrs Buthelezi,' she said. 'I'll tell my grandmother that.'

'When you do, tell her that you too should be in school. You're a promising student, Lydia. I would like to see you do well.'

'But what about Kesi?' Lydia asked.

'I'll do my best to protect her.'

Lydia nodded as the teacher strode away. She was pleased with herself that she had spoken out, and to hear that she was 'a promising student'. She would tell her grandmother, and say that she must go and talk to the Head about the fees.

'She won't be able to stop us from going to school if we're allowed to go for free,' Lydia said to herself. 'And I'm sure if I work harder at home, I'll be able to go to at least some of the classes.'

She walked as quickly as she could, especially when she came to the place where the strange man had spoken to her. She breathed a sigh of relief to discover that he wasn't there. Two of the villagers, who were sweeping their yards, turned away when they saw her. Another, Mrs Sibiya, who was hanging out her washing, asked how she was. Lydia smiled, saying that she was doing well, and just at that moment she meant it. Mrs Sibiya told her to wait, disappeared indoors and reappeared with a small bowl of beans.

'Here,' she said, 'take this. It's all I can spare, but it will help a bit and your mother was a good friend to me. I wouldn't like to see you going hungry.'

Lydia said thank you several times before she felt she had expressed her gratitude enough to continue on her way.

Choose your friends carefully, my child. Be sure their heads are wise and their hearts warm.

Lydia had a skip in her step now. The day had turned itself round and she felt a bit more hopeful by the time she reached the door of their rondavel. She was about to go in, ready to tell Joe the good news, when she heard a man's voice coming from round the back. She stopped for a moment to listen. Joe was talking to someone. The voice sounded vaguely familiar, but she couldn't place it. She peered round the side of the rondavel, and there was the man who had thrown a stone across her path. He was digging in their garden, his shirt thrown over the branch of a tree. Joe and Kesi were close by, pulling at the weeds.

Lydia was so appalled that it took her a moment to find her breath. 'What do you think you're doing?' she demanded at last.

The man looked up and grinned. 'Ah,' he said, 'we meet again.'

Kesi ran over and grabbed Lydia's hand. 'His name's Mr Theki and he's helping us to dig the garden and we found an enormous worm and three potatoes. He said he'd read me a story and he doesn't mind if I touch him.'

'Jabu Theki. You can call me Jabu,' the man said, wiping his hand on his trousers and stretching it out for Lydia to shake. 'Perhaps we can start again.'

'Please leave our property, Mr Theki,' Lydia ordered. 'We don't want you here.'

Joe stood up abruptly from his weeding. 'Don't be like that, Lydia. He's helping us.'

'We don't need his help,' said Lydia.

'Yes we do,' argued Joe. 'We can't do everything by ourselves.'

'Look, I don't want to cause any problems,' said the man. He picked up his shirt and threw it over his shoulder, took hold of the fork he had been using and made his way towards Lydia.

She wished he had put his shirt on, and turned her head away as he came close to her.

'No offence intended,' he said, leaning towards her, then he marched off down the road, whistling loudly.

Lydia dropped Kesi's hand and took the bowl of beans inside. Joe followed her and stood in the doorway.

'He was being nice to us. Why were you so rude to him?' he grumbled.

'Because I don't like him and I don't want him here.'

'He wasn't doing any harm, and you know we need help.'

'Not from him, not from a stranger,' Lydia said firmly. 'Not when we don't know anything about him. You don't understand, Joe. Anyway, I spoke to Mrs Buthelezi and she thinks we won't have to pay school fees because we're – because of Baba and Mama. She says Grandma needs to talk to the Head to sort it out.'

'Grandma won't do that, I bet.'

'If I'm really nice to her, I'm sure she will.'

'I'm going now then,' said Joe. 'You coming, Kes?'

Kesi shook her head. 'Don't like school,' she mumbled.

'Go with him, Kes. It'll be all right. Mrs Buthelezi promised. And at least they'll feed you there.'

'Come on, Kes,' said Joe. 'I'll give you a piggyback.'

Kesi squealed with delight as he picked her up and cantered round the room before galloping out of the door. Lydia watched them cavorting down the road, then turned to the yams and beans and tried to decide what to cook for their evening meal.

Chapter 4

Take a good look at this photo, Lydia. It's how I want you to remember me. I was well then. See the wide smile on my face and my handsome figure. OK, those hips were carrying too many extra pounds, but two babies had already passed through them, and your brother, Joe, he was a BIG one. I was good-looking, eh? Your baba thought so. He was alive then, we lived in the town and we were having fun. We had such fun, didn't we, Lydia? I want you to have fun again. I want you to remember how it feels to laugh and laugh until your ribs are about to burst. Like when we went to market and that rascally cockerel of ours escaped. He led us such a merry dance, skedaddling up and down the street, in and out of the houses, squawk, squawk, squawking, his legs pumping like pistons. I think he knew he was for the pot and he was getting out of town. Your father threw himself at him and ripped his trousers, but he caught enough of that plucky bird's proud tail to halt his progress. Your father held him tight under his arm, looked him straight in the eye and said, 'Naughty cockerel.' Well, that cockerel, he pecked him hard on the nose and it was your father's turn to squawk. Baba loosened his hold, the cockerel escaped again and that's the last we saw of him.

And do you remember when we went to the sea? We were so lucky to be able to do that. We watched the fishermen untangling their nets and sorting their catch. We saw pelicans plunging into the waves and re-emerging with their bills full of fish. We built a mansion in the sand with our bare hands, laughing that one day we would live in a mansion and have servants and our own swimming pool and someone else would build it for us. Dreams are what help us through our lives, Lydia. Don't let people steal your dreams. People always try to steal your dreams.

Do you remember too that we buried your baba in the sand? He lay down and we shovelled sand over him so that only his toes and his face were showing. And then he sneezed. He sneezed so hard that his knees and his head catapulted upwards and the sand flew over Joe, who was sitting beside him eating a piece of melon. Poor Joe, he howled like a jackal in the mouth of a lioness when he saw what had happened to his melon. He shook his hands in anger and the melon landed – PLOP – in the middle of your father's belly. The look of shock on your father's face made me howl with laughter, then you joined in, and Baba, and even little Joe. That was a day, that was.

Lydia wondered if she would ever see the sea again. They were celebrating her mother's birthday that day. It seemed so long ago. They had travelled there in their father's truck, she and Joe in the back, bumping along on the red, dry, rutted road, singing silly songs at the tops of their voices. She smiled to herself at the thought of her father singing. He was always out of tune but it didn't stop him. The more they put their fingers in their ears, the louder he became. 'It's not my singing that's the problem,' he would chuckle. 'It's your hearing.'

Lydia remembered the last time he tried to sing. He was sitting up in bed, feeling a bit better, he had told them. He managed a few notes, thin and scratchy, then he started to cough and couldn't stop. He coughed a lot after that, and he never sang again.

'The sea, think about the sea,' Lydia said to herself.

The sea that hushed and roared, shimmered and frowned, bubbled and boiled. The sea that tickled your toes then pulled your legs from underneath you, playful then angry, kindly then dangerous. What faraway places lay beyond it? What were the people like who lived in the places beyond? Were there girls like her, girls on their own looking after brothers, looking after sisters, missing their parents, dreaming about the sea and wondering what it was like on the other side? Were there people dying in that land beyond — not dying because they were old, but dying because they were ill and couldn't be helped? Was it like that all over the world?

Lydia shivered and tried again to push the black thoughts away. She stared at the photograph. Her mother looked so happy. She was pretty too, not in a flowery way, but her high cheekbones were striking, her eyes soft and wide, and her smile revealed a gap between her two front teeth that gave her a mischievous air. She had been mischievous sometimes. Lydia could see her now, dropping a crab in the pocket of her father's shorts and warning Joe not to give the game away.

Do I look like her? Lydia wondered.

She jumped up from the chair and gazed in the mirror. She traced her cheekbones with her finger. They were flatter. Her eyes were closer set and her teeth less prominent. She certainly didn't look mischievous. She seemed rather sombre, and her eyes didn't light up even when she tried to pretend she was laughing. Her skin was dull, while in the photograph her mother's had a healthy glow.

Mama was prettier, she thought to herself, *until she got ill. Kesi looks like Mama.*

'You are your father's daughter,' her mother used to tell Lydia. She tried to remember her father's face, but it was so long now since she had last seen him that she found it difficult to recall his features. She could see his broken front tooth, but the fleshy features round it drifted off into vague shadows. And then the skeleton reappeared, the skeleton he had turned into just before he died. Her mother had turned into a skeleton too. The soft, wide eyes had become bloodshot and ringed with grey, the cheekbones had stood out even more prominently as the plump cheeks became sunken, the smile had faded with the effort of pretence. Lydia had sat and held the skin and bone of her mother's hand while the last whispers of breath left her lips.

Lydia took one final look at the photograph, tried to fix it in her memory, then put it back in the box with all the other things her mother had assembled for her children. She noticed that the little book her mother had struggled to put together for Joe was missing and realised that he too must be seeking comfort in it. She determined to try harder to take care of his needs. He was doing his best to help her, even if he had been a bit grumpy recently. She tidied up the pots and pans, brought the mattress back indoors, fitted the sheet over it, then, satisfied that their home was as tidy as her mother would have left it, set off in the direction of her grandmother's house.

It was a long time since she had been there. They had never felt particularly welcome but, when their father died, the old woman had made it clear that her home was out of bounds to them. She would come to their rondavel, but they would not be invited back. Not only that, but she removed from their own home everything that she considered belonged to their father. Lydia's mother had tried to stop her, arguing that some of the things she was laying claim to had belonged to her own parents, but in the end she gave up. 'Do they put food on the table?' she said to Lydia. 'Do they make the vegetables in the garden grow? Do they make the sun shine brighter in our lives? If your grandmother wants them so much, let her have them.' She regretted it later, when she found that she too was ill – when she realised that she had given away things she would have liked to put in her memory box for her children.

Lydia's grandmother lived on the other side of the village, over three kilometres away, in a house with a tiled roof and its own supply of water. She was always complaining about how hard her life was and how her husband had left her ill provided for, but she had a television that worked and enough money to hire someone to look after her land, which extended to more than a hectare. As Lydia drew near, she noticed that the house had a new front door and that her property had been newly painted.

The door opened. Lydia's courage left her and she turned ready to flee, until she saw that it wasn't her grandmother but a young girl from the village. The girl walked quickly across the yard before emptying the bucket she was carrying on to the neat rows of vegetables that stretched away from the house.

'Annie?' Lydia called.

The girl glanced up briefly and looked uneasy.

'What are you doing here, Annie?' Lydia asked.

'I work here,' the girl replied.

'Why aren't you going to school?'

'Because we have no money since Baba died. Mama needs me to work. I must go in now. Mrs Motsie will get cross. Shall I tell her you're here?'

Lydia shook her head and watched as Annie fled around the back of the house. She wanted a few moments to compose herself. She was upset by Annie's appearance. The young girl looked so thin and fragile, scarcely able to lift the bucket of water, and her face was etched with misery.

Is she ill? Lydia wondered, but she was certain her grandmother wouldn't employ Annie if she thought there was anything wrong with her. She wondered, then, how much her grandmother was paying her, and if she was kind to her. She had her doubts. Or was it just her own family the old woman treated badly?

Lydia took a deep breath and walked up to the door. She knocked and waited, aware that her heart was beating wildly and the palms of her hands were damp with sweat.

Joe and Kesi will need your strength.

Through an open window, she heard her grandmother ordering Annie to continue with her work, then a figure appeared at the door. Lydia took in the look of shock on her grandmother's face, before she lowered her eyes and apologised for the intrusion.

'What's happened? What do you want?' Grandma Motsie frowned.

Lydia took a deep breath. 'It's about the school. I've spoken to the teacher. We may not need to pay. She wants you to go and talk to the Head.'

The old woman looked furious. 'So you think we need charity now, do you?' she snapped.

'No, but it's the same for all children who haven't got parents.' Lydia still found it difficult to say the word 'orphan'.

'I don't care what it's like for other children. I'm not having people pointing fingers at my family and saying we're paupers.'

It didn't make any sense, what she was saying. Lydia began to feel desperate. 'Please, Grandma,' she begged, 'please go and talk to them. No one needs to know if we can't pay. Joe loves school and he's doing so well, and Kesi needs to learn to read and write.'

'What a waste of time that would be,' her grandmother snorted. 'And who do you think is going to pay for new uniforms when the old ones wear out? It'll be obvious even to a fool that the money's run out if you turn up in tatters.'

Lydia could feel tears welling up. She blinked them back angrily. 'No one's going to think you're poor,' she murmured. 'Not when you're employing servants.'

'How dare you, young lady,' Grandma Motsie exploded. 'Are you questioning how I spend my money?'

Lydia bit her tongue, staring hard at the ground.

'Get out! Get out, and don't come back.'

Lydia turned and ran as fast as she could. Behind her, she heard the door slam.

Chapter 5

I want you to know about your family so that when you have a family yourself you can tell them where they came from and be proud. I'll tell you first about my mother and my father, Grandma and Grandpa Kaleni. Do you remember them?

Do I remember them? Lydia wondered.

She had some vague recollection of a tall man with great big hands, a prickly chin and a laugh that made her jump every time it broke out. Was it her grandfather? She thought she had liked that man, especially when he had picked her up and put her on his shoulders, then galloped with her round and round the house. Whose house was that? Was it where Grandma and Grandpa Kaleni lived, or where she had lived herself, with her mother and father, when they first moved to the town and where they had been living when the big storm hit? She tried to picture it, but the only memory she had was of a large rocking chair in which the man used to sit smoking a pipe, and in which she used to fall asleep on his lap. Did that belong with the other memories she had of a tiny garden with a deep well, a rusty old sewing machine and the smell of sweet potatoes cooking?

My mother, Grandma Kaleni, was so beautiful that all the young men in the village wanted to marry her. She chose your grandfather because of his fine biceps. 'When I saw those,' she said, 'I knew they would hug me like a bear, and I wanted to be hugged like a bear.' When she was serious, she told me that it was because she knew he was kind, and kindness is a virtue that is all too rare. It was his honesty as well, she told me. He may not have been blessed with an enormous brain, but at least she could trust him.

He was always there for us, your grandfather. He worked all day at the sugar mill, then he came home and kicked a ball with me and my brother, or tried to help us with our schoolwork, or read to us, stumbling and stuttering over every sentence. Sometimes he plucked stories from the wind and they were always the best. He may have struggled

45

with words on a page, but his imagination took us to far-away worlds. He would sit in his rocking chair, pipe in hand, and we would sit by his feet and listen. In the kitchen, your grandmother would perform magic with rice and vegetables – quietly, because she would be listening too. Once in a while she would cuss when, like us, she became so transported by his tales that she allowed something to burn.

You just wouldn't believe the smells that wafted out through that kitchen window. Grandma Kaleni was the finest cook in the whole of Africa. She must have been – well, we thought so. Sometimes I wondered if it wasn't her cooking your father courted and not me! And in her garden she performed miracles. No matter how hostile the weather, no matter how seemingly barren the ground, she could coax even the most reluctant plant, the most stubborn vegetable to grow and flourish. We were lucky to be able to eat so well, we knew that. There were plenty of people at that time who struggled to beat off starvation. Your grandmother would have put food on their tables too, had she been able.

Lydia walked to the door and looked out at the garden. Could she do that? Could she do what Grandma Kaleni had done and perform miracles? How? She sat down on the ground and gazed through the mass of weeds that had choked their vegetables. How could she do anything when she couldn't even get their fork to dig through the parched earth?

They were so excited when you were born, Lydia. Grandpa Kaleni did a mad dance in the garden and your grandma sang a lullaby. She sang songs to you every single day after that. She had a voice that sounded as if it had been steeped in honey, it was so sweet and mellow. You would lie in your crib and look up at her with your eyes wide, waggling your arms and legs, until your eyelids began to droop and your little body stilled.

I remember the songs, thought Lydia, *not from then, not from when I was a baby, but from when we all sang together; Grandma and Grandpa Kaleni, Mother and Father. Even Joe joined in.*

She smiled as she recalled her brother trying to clap his hands together, his nose dribbling, his lips lisping. Poor Joe, he only knew his grandparents for a short time before they died, one after the other, within the space of a year. Kesi had never known them at all. 'Your grandmother died of pneumonia, then your grandfather died of a broken heart,' their mother told them. 'They just couldn't live without each other.'

Lydia wondered what it would be like to love somebody so much that you couldn't live without them. And then she wondered why she hadn't died when her mother was taken from her, because surely nobody could love another person as much as she loved her mother. And her father. She loved her father too, though she couldn't help hating him sometimes, whatever her mother said.

The sun was beating down. Lydia knew she should get on with the chores, but she couldn't seem to find the energy. The chores were there every day, making their demands. She was tired of being at their beck and call. So what if she ignored them just for one day? She watched a beetle scuttle across the dry earth and disappear under a heap of rotting food scraps. She waited to see if it would reappear, before turning another page of her mother's book.

Every single new word you learned, every single small step you took was a matter for rejoicing where Grandma and Grandpa Kaleni were concerned. It was as if they had never seen such things before. I had to remind them that I was a baby once and I had been pretty clever too. They argued that it was a long time ago, and that I had been too much of a pain in the bottom to give them much reason to rejoice. I caught them winking, so I knew they weren't serious, and I couldn't help smiling at the way they clucked and cooed over you. It was just the same when Joe was born, except that the minute he took his first steps Grandpa Kaleni put a ball in front of his feet. When Joe kicked it, by accident as he stumbled forward, your grandfather boasted that he had natural talent and would soon be playing for the national team!

We were such a happy family back then. Your grandparents adored your baba, you know. They trusted him to be a good husband and a kind father, which he was, Lydia, most of the time. If only his mother had taken to me just as enthusiastically. His father, Grandpa Motsie, was friendly enough. He was a quiet man, do you remember? The complete opposite of Grandpa Kaleni, yet they got on well, the two of them.

Grandpa Motsie had smoked a pipe. They had talked a lot together, Lydia remembered, *about politics and history.*
   She and Joe had thought him rather dull because he never played with them, though he watched them and

smiled sometimes, a secret smile that never broke out into laughter however much Grandpa Kaleni roared at their antics. He did everything his wife demanded and seemed devoted to her. Lydia was puzzled by that, because Grandma Motsie seemed to treat her husband so harshly.

'You won't even begin to understand the dynamics of adult relationships until you are an adult yourself,' her mother had told her with a grin, when she questioned why her grandfather put up with it. 'And even then you won't be able to make head nor tail. For them, it works. However, if I treated your father like that, he would be after me with a machete!'

Lydia smiled. The worst violence she had ever witnessed her father inflict on her mother was when he galloped after her and rapped her bottom with a wooden spoon, and that was because she stole a carrot from a meal he was preparing. Sometimes, she thought, her parents had been like two schoolchildren the way they larked around. They'd owned a pig once. One day, her father had gone down on all fours next to the pig and pretended to snuffle around for food. Her mother went out into the yard with a bowl of slops and tipped them all over him. She couldn't imagine Grandma and Grandpa Motsie being playful together. She couldn't imagine Grandma Motsie loving anybody, and yet she had loved her husband and her son.

Why can't she love us? Lydia wanted to know.

But it was too late now. Her grandmother had washed her hands of them. They were on their own. She closed the book and took it back to the box under the bed.

'We're on our own, Mama,' she whispered. 'I wish I knew what to do now.'

Chapter 6

Lydia was in the garden when Joe and Kesi arrived back from school. She had spent the previous four hours pulling at the weeds and trying to dig out their roots. The prongs of the fork had bent against the solid earth and she had hurled it away in frustration.

'How does anything grow in this?' she muttered over and over. 'How does something as soft as a weed push its way through something so hard?' She stood up and stretched her back as her brother and sister clattered into the yard.

'Liddy, Liddy, Liddy,' cried Kesi. 'I like school now. Mrs Buthelezi gave me a gold star for my reading.'

'Well done, Kes,' smiled Lydia, giving her a hug.

'And I didn't mind sitting in the corner because Mrs Buthelezi says it's the best place in the room because the sun shines on it.'

'That's good,' said Lydia. 'How's your day been, Joe?'

'I only scored two goals in football practice, didn't I?' he said loftily.

'That's great, Joe.'

'I'm the best in the team.'

'And the most big-headed,' Lydia grinned.

'It's not big-headed. It's true,' he protested.

'Joe got told off for calling Nkosi a rude name, didn't you, Joe, and for fi—' said Kesi.

'And I came bottom in a maths test, but who cares?' interrupted Joe, shrugging his shoulders. 'It wasn't important.'

'I care,' said Lydia. 'Maths is important, and why did you call Nkosi a rude name?'

'Because he was saying things about us and he deserved it. When's Grandma going to see the Head?'

Lydia looked at his anxious face and couldn't, at that moment, tell him the truth. She averted her eyes as she replied, 'Soon, I hope. She's a bit busy.'

'And we're not important enough for her to put us first? You'd think she would run all the way there since it means she won't have to pay for us,' Joe grumbled.

'Grandma can't run,' giggled Kesi. 'She says she's got old legs that don't work any more, and she wobbles.'

'I bet she'd run fast if someone offered to give her money,' said Joe.

'Don't be disrespectful, please, Joe,' said Lydia.

Joe grunted and turned to go indoors. As he did, Lydia noticed the back of his trousers. 'Joe, you've got a big hole in your trousers,' she scolded. 'How did that get there?'

'*I* know,' said Kesi importantly.

'And you're not to tell,' Lydia said quickly.

'I caught it on a fence,' Joe answered, before disappearing indoors.

Lydia wiped her hands down the front of the old skirt she was wearing. She wished there was some way in which she could keep the harsh realities of their situation from Joe and Kesi. They were still so young. She hated the way Joe was suddenly becoming grumpy and truculent. It wasn't like him. He had always been so agreeable and willing. If only something good would happen for him, something *really* good, like being chosen to captain the school football team or finding maths easy. She smiled at the thought that he might ever find maths easy. He just didn't have the sort of brain to fathom out puzzles and in that he took after their father. When she tried to help, she became almost as frustrated as he did, because she couldn't understand

54

why he found it so difficult. Joe's strength lay in subjects like geography and biology, and he was passionate about those, whereas Lydia found them dull.

She followed her brother indoors, Kesi trotting behind her. 'I'm determined to sort the garden out,' she said. 'Will you help?'

She looked searchingly at Joe, who shrugged his shoulders. 'I can't do it on my own,' she continued.

'I'll help,' squealed Kesi.

'That's good,' said Lydia, giving her sister a squeeze. 'What about you, Joe?'

'It would have been done by now if you'd let that man help,' mumbled Joe.

'Yes,' she snapped. 'Life will be so much better for all of us if we sell our souls.' She grabbed hold of the sweet potatoes that were still sitting on the table, and threw them across the garden. 'But we're not going to do that, do you hear me?' Without waiting for a response, she stormed out through the door and began to pull at the weeds again, while her hot tears fell to the ground. She heard scuffles behind her and knew that Joe and Kesi were standing there watching her. She tore out another handful and flung it away in despair.

'Don't, Liddy,' Joe's voice reached her. 'Course I'll help. Don't get angry.'

She turned and gazed at him, taking in the look of shock that paralysed his face.

'I'm sorry, all right?' he said simply. 'Shall I heat up the stew?' He didn't wait for her to answer but went straight back inside.

Lydia listened to the clattering of pans as she tried to compose herself.

We were such a happy family back then.

'Joe,' she called.

His face appeared round the door.

'I'm sorry as well,' she said. 'I'll fetch some water, then after we've eaten we could play a game of umphuco, if you like, before it gets too dark.'

'Maybe,' he replied.

'Let me play too!' cried Kesi. She ran into the garden and began to collect a pile of stones. Lydia was struck again by how skinny her little sister looked, but she seemed healthy enough.

'Food first, and lots of it for you, Kes,' she told her. 'Now go and help Joe lay the table.'

She watched Kesi rush indoors, then set off through the hedge and along the dusty track towards the water pipe. As she approached it, she saw another girl of about her own age filling up a large pitcher. It was Mandisa, one of her best friends from school, who had been kind to her when her mother died, but whom she hadn't seen for several weeks. She was glad to bump into her. She needed to talk to someone her own age.

'Mandisa,' she called out. 'How are you, Mandisa?'

The girl looked up and waved briefly, but didn't answer. Lydia reached her and took her arm. 'I've missed you,' she said. 'How's school?'

'I'm not going,' Mandisa replied. 'My mother's sick and my father's left us. I don't want to leave her alone, and Simba has got a job.'

Simba was Mandisa's sixteen-year-old brother. Lydia was shocked to hear that he had a job because the family had planned for him to go to university. She looked at her friend's face. It was pinched with anxiety.

'How long has your mother been sick?' she asked quietly.

'On and off for a while,' said Mandisa. 'She kept getting sores in her mouth and then she started coughing a lot. Now she's tired all the time. She'll get better though, I know she will. It's not like with your mama. It's not the same as that. She just needs to rest up and eat a bit more. It's because she's been so angry at Baba for leaving that she feels so weak.'

Lydia bit her lip. She didn't want to argue, but she knew that the symptoms her friend had described were the same as her own mother's. And she was sure that her friend knew it too, deep down, but didn't want to face it. Why would anyone believe the worst when there still might be hope?

'Why did your father go?' she ventured to ask.

'Because he's a coward and a monster,' Mandisa hissed. 'He ran away the minute Mama first got ill. Just didn't come back. He said he was going to work, at the mills, like he always did. But he didn't go to work. He packed some clothes, took all our savings from the drawer, and people say he's got a job in a different province. I hope he rots there.'

At least our baba stayed, Lydia thought to herself. *At least he faced up to what he did.*

Don't ever hate your father, Lydia. We talked about that over and over and I know that sometimes you wanted to hate him so much for what he did. He wasn't all bad though. He was weak, like so many of our men, and he was foolish for believing that he was untouchable. He paid the price too, didn't he? I didn't hate him. I watched him suffer, not just in his body but in his head, and I listened to him saying sorry a hundred

58

times. When he discovered that he had passed his illness on to me, and perhaps to little Kesi, he was like a child who wanted to be forgiven so badly and to have his hurt taken away. I forgave him because I loved him once, and I know that love can easily turn to hate, but hatred is destructive. I didn't let it in because I didn't want it to destroy me, and I don't want it to destroy you.

'Perhaps he was scared,' Lydia said.

'Who cares if he was scared? We're all scared, but it doesn't mean we're running away and leaving the people we're supposed to love. Don't make excuses for him, Lydia. It's because of him Simba's had to leave school and take a job. He's got to keep us now, and it's not fair.'

I've got to keep Joe and Kesi, thought Lydia. *That's not fair either and I haven't got an older brother.*

She scolded herself straight away for comparing her circumstances to Mandisa's. Mandisa's mother was sick and Mandisa needed her support, not pointless comparisons.

'If there's anything I can do,' she offered.

Mandisa shrugged her shoulders. 'I'll be all right,' she said, 'as soon as Mama's better. My grandmother's helping too. She wants me to go back to school. Are you going back?'

It was Lydia's turn to shrug. 'Maybe,' she said. She wanted to tell Mandisa about Grandma Motsie, but it felt disloyal and she was scared her grandmother would find out if she told tales. 'There's always so much to do.' Then she added, though she didn't know where the thought had come from, 'Sometimes I feel like running away.'

'What, on your own?'

'With Joe and Kesi.'

'Where would you go?'

'I don't know. Just somewhere. Somewhere better.'

'What if there isn't anywhere better?' Mandisa sniffed.

'There must be, mustn't there?'

'If you're rich, I suppose.' Mandisa took hold of her pitcher and lifted it on to her head. 'We'll never be rich if we don't go to school,' she said as she began to walk away.

Lydia filled her own jug and set off back home. Something about the conversation with Mandisa had sparked a deep longing in her, a longing to be somewhere else, to be someone else. To be amongst people who were full of the joy of life, not haunted by the

60

shadow of death. To be able to dream of a future that could become a glorious reality, instead of watching it shatter at every turn of thought. To be free of the responsibility of looking after Joe and Kesi. Lydia stopped in her tracks. How could she long for that? They were her brother and sister. She loved them. She hurried on before further traitorous thoughts could trouble her.

Chapter 7

'Do you think Grandma will go to and see the Head today?' Joe asked as soon as he woke the next morning.

'If she won't, I'll go myself,' muttered Lydia quietly to herself. She dragged herself out of bed and went to the door. It was drizzling with rain, enough to make the air humid but not enough to loosen up the soil and persuade the vegetables to grow.

'What will you say?'

'I'll say that the government says we have to go to school because school is important, but we don't have any money to pay.'

'And you'll say that I'm in the football team and the team needs me.'

'I'll say that you need to be in school because your maths is poo.'

'It's not poo, it's just –'

'Wee!' squealed Kesi, who woke up at that moment and leapt out of bed. 'It's just wee! I didn't wee, Lydia, look – the bed's dry.'

'Well done, Kes,' grinned Lydia. She was genuinely delighted for her sister. She was grateful too that it meant one less chore to do that day.

'Are we going to school?' Kesi asked.

'Yes, you're going to school.'

'And will I sit in the sunny corner again?'

Lydia ruffled her hair. 'If that's where you want to sit, then I expect that's where you'll be sitting, and I'll pray for the sun to come out.'

'Will you read with me when I come home? Mrs Buthelezi says we're to read at home every day and I forgot yesterday because of the umphuco.'

'Then I'll have to remember for you,' said Lydia, 'and I'm sure Joe will help as well.'

Joe pulled a face. 'I will if you help me with my poo.'

'Yuck, yuck, yuck!' screeched Kesi. 'Nobody wants to help you with that!'

'That will do,' Lydia said firmly. 'Come on, Joe, go and fetch the water or we'll all be late.'

Joe picked up the jug, turned it upside down on his head, much to the amusement of Kesi, who picked up the bowl that had contained the beans and put it on her head. Together they traipsed off into the rain, singing at the tops of their voices. Lydia smiled at their antics and was happy that the day had started well.

'I can do this, Mama,' she whispered under her breath. 'I will make you proud.'

There was still food left from the night before. Lydia heated it on their tiny gas stove and planned her day ahead. She would apologise to Grandma Motsie for being rude and disrespectful, and ask her again, politely, if she would please go to see the Head. She would ask her too if she could spare a little money so that she could buy some more vegetable seeds. And she would need to ask for some cotton so that she could sew up Joe's trousers. There wasn't any left in her mother's sewing box, though she didn't know where it had all gone. She would offer to do some chores for her grandmother to show that she was trying her hardest to make amends. She could offer to do her shopping, and when she went to the shop she could buy the seeds and see if Mr Luthuli, the owner, had a spade she could borrow. And if he didn't, there must be someone in the village who would help, especially if she promised to return it straight away.

She laid her brother and sister's uniforms on the bed, ready for them to change into as soon as they came back. When she went round the bed to fetch Joe's shoes in case they needed cleaning, she found his memory book. It was open and a faded family photograph was lying on top. Lydia picked up the photograph. She gazed at the smiling faces of her mother and father, who were standing in between Grandma and Grandpa Kaleni on one side and Grandma and Grandpa Motsie on the other. Lydia herself, aged about six, was sitting on a chair in front of them, a young baby wrapped in a blanket lying across her lap. It was Joe, she knew that. She had seen the photograph many times before. But it was different this time. There was a hole through Grandma Motsie's face.

A ragged hole that let in the light. Lydia traced round it with her finger. All the other grown-ups in the picture had passed away. Grandma Motsie had been wiped out. By Joe? It had to be Joe. Did he hate her that much? She couldn't blame him. He must have guessed that she had refused to go to the school. He must be hurting so badly behind the brave front he presented to the world. She stooped to return the photograph and noticed something else. It was Joe's maths test. The piece of paper was covered with red crosses. He really was terrible at maths, and he cared more than he was admitting.

Footsteps outside made her rush to the kitchen and busy herself with plates and spoons. Her brother and sister came through the door, Joe carrying a full jug of water on his head, Kesi, tongue out, carefully carrying the bowl, which had only the tiniest drop of water left in it.

'I got some too, but it kept going splosh on the ground,' she giggled.

'More like down my legs,' Joe said.

'Well done anyway,' said Lydia, 'and thanks, Joe.' She caught hold of his hand and squeezed it.

He looked at her curiously. 'It was all right this morning,' he said. 'We didn't have any trouble.'

Lydia was relieved, but she wanted more than anything to be able to take him aside, put her arms round him and tell him to leave the worrying to her. There wasn't time. The morning was always too busy. The minute Joe and Kesi had had something to eat and put on their uniforms, they had to fly.

'Work hard,' she said to them as they hurried off.

'And you,' said Joe.

Lydia watched them disappear into the distance.

Are they all right? she wondered.

She was sure their hearts must be heavy above those skipping feet.

She dug her mother's memory box out from underneath the bed. She wanted to steep herself in her mother's words before she continued with the day. But first she wanted to look at some of the things her mother had collected over the years and which she had gathered together in the box. Lydia picked up photographs of family and friends, studied them carefully and tried to remember who each person was. She fingered bits of material from old clothes. There was a piece from her mother's wedding dress and a ribbon that she herself had worn when she was Kesi's age. She traced the outlines of leaves and flowers that Grandma Kaleni had pasted on to pages of handmade parchment. She felt the rough clay of a pot her great-grandmother had made. She smiled at spidery drawings, the work of Grandpa Kaleni and her father, both of whom thought they were undiscovered artists. And then there were her own colourful daubs on random pieces of paper.

Lydia was so engrossed with what she was doing that she failed to hear footsteps approaching. She jumped with fright when a dark shadow fell across the doorway.

'And well you might look startled,' Grandma Motsie's voice shattered her thoughts.

Lydia sprang to her feet and tried to push the box back under the bed with her feet.

'Have you nothing more important to do than to wallow in the past?'

Lydia didn't know what to say.

'The yard needs sweeping and the rubbish needs clearing. You insult our family name by neglecting your home. Anyway, I've come to tell you that I'm prepared to forgive you for your insolence yesterday. I'm sure you didn't mean it, and I expect you are keen to apologise so that we can move on.'

The old woman paused and stared at Lydia.

If you find yourself without money, Lydia, ask Grandma Motsie. She has all the money I saved for you and plenty of her own hidden away. She won't refuse her own grandchildren. Don't be too proud to ask.

'I am very sorry, Grandma Motsie. I know you are trying your hardest for us and we appreciate your help. If only we could find some way to keep Joe and Kesi in school.'

Lydia waited nervously for her grandmother's reaction.

'That's why I am here, despite your outburst yesterday, and I accept your apology provided that it is meant.'

'I do mean it, Grandma. I was hoping that you might also be able to help us buy some vegetable seeds so that we can fend for ourselves.'

'You've failed so far,' sniffed the old woman. 'And how do you think all this is going to be funded?'

Lydia looked at her pleadingly. 'I thought perhaps I could do some errands for you.'

'Yes, that's precisely what you can do. Or rather, you can work for me. I've sacked that silly girl, Annie, so you can take her place, starting tomorrow. You won't be paid, but I will go and talk with the school.'

Lydia saw immediately that what her grandmother was proposing would not cost her anything. The government would pay for Joe and Kesi's schooling, and she would have Lydia's services for free. All of a sudden, Grandma Motsie wasn't worried about her reputation.

'What about the uniforms?' was all Lydia could think to say.

'I'm sure there's a lot more wear in them, and I

believe that because you are orphans the government will pay for replacements, since I cannot afford to myself.'

'I really need some cotton to mend Joe's trousers when he comes home.'

Lydia was struggling not to burst into tears as she took on board the full import of what her grandmother was proposing. If she agreed to it, she would never be able to go back to school herself. If she didn't agree, none of them would be able to go to school, unless she defied her grandmother and went to visit the Head herself. But Grandma Motsie was a powerful influence in the village and could make life very difficult for them, even more difficult than it was already.

'How will I be able to look after Joe and Kesi if I'm working for you?' Lydia asked, trying not to sound too doubtful.

'Of course I shall allow you to return home in time to sort out their needs. I am not entirely lacking in understanding.'

'No, Grandma, of course not.'

'And I shall do what I can to feed you all, provided that you work hard enough.'

'I'll work very hard,' Lydia said firmly.

'Good. We're agreed then. I shall expect you at my house at six o'clock tomorrow morning, ready to serve breakfast.'

Without waiting for a reply, Grandma Motsie turned and waddled away up the path.

Chapter 8

What do I hope for you, Lydia? What should be the first thing? Happiness, I think. A big happiness, as well as all the minute happinesses that pop up ready for you to seize if you are watching out for them. When you find that big happiness, then it means you will have reached a point in your life where everything that matters to you is going well. It means that you are comfortable with who you are, what you have achieved and what you are achieving. It means that the people you care about are happy too, because how can you be happy if someone you care about is sad? It means that you can wake up in the morning and smile on the world, even if the sky is heavy with clouds. I want that so much for you, Lydia, and for Joe and little Kesi. The road to big happiness will be hard. It is always hard. But when you find it, leap upon it as if it were the rarest and most precious thing on earth and hold on to it so tightly that it cannot slip away.

We have had big happinesses. We tried to seize all the little happinesses too. And we have had sadness. Deep sadness. Nobody passes through this life without experiencing sadness. You have had more than your fair share for your young years, and so have many of the children in our village. You will deserve your big happiness when you find it, all of you. Until then, try not to despair and never –

A sudden draught blew out the candle.

'– never give up,' Lydia muttered to herself.

There were no more matches left in the box. She lay in the dark and listened to the untroubled breathing of Joe and Kesi. They were still going to school and they were happy. She had made them believe that if she worked for Grandma Motsie it would be a good thing. She had even managed to believe it herself, until the evening had drawn in, night had fallen, the chatter of her brother and sister had died away, and she was left with nothing but her thoughts. Black thoughts with no light behind them. She didn't want to work for her grandmother.

She wanted to go to school. She wanted one day to have a good job. If she didn't have a good job, how would she ever find her big happiness? If she worked for Grandma Motsie, the prospect of finding even minute happinesses disappeared.

She tried to stop herself thinking like that. She was helping Joe and Kesi, just as her mother had asked her, and that should surely make her happy. If it didn't, was it because she was being selfish? She determined that she would do her best both to please her grandmother and to protect her brother and sister from any problems she might have working for her.

You may have to become someone else to survive, Lydia. You're a dreamer, and dreamers can fashion roads to Eden, but life has thrown you a challenge that will mean you have to face reality with your eyes wide open. Fix your dreams in the quiet of your mind and never let them go, but be awake to the demands each day will make on you.

Lydia woke earlier than usual the next morning. It was quite dark outside and the cicadas were still singing. There were shuffling sounds from nearby homesteads, as the village men prepared to set off for work in the sugar mills. A cockerel crowed from somewhere distant and another, much closer, began a rival announcement of the coming of the day.

Such a strange sound, Lydia thought. *Such an ugly sound to be woken by. Not as bad, though, as being woken by a donkey – EEE-AWW.*

Kesi stirred in her sleep and wiped her nose on Lydia's arm. On the other side of her, Joe kicked out a leg, muttered something incomprehensible, flailed an arm, then fell silent again.

Is he playing football in his sleep? Lydia wondered.

She slipped quietly out of bed and tiptoed across to the door. A gentle breeze buffed her cheeks as she stared up at the shifting sky. There were so many colours. She watched as streaks of pink and orange were lit up by flashes of light, closed down by surges of grey, then reawoken by the emerging sun. What sort of day was it going to be? Would the sun break through or was the grey too bullying? A sudden movement in the garden made her jump. She let out a loud squeal when a black shape ran across in front of her. It had gone again almost as soon as she saw it, and she quickly realised that it was probably only a dog. But the fright stayed with her and knocked what little confidence she had built up to approach this new chapter in her life.

She went back indoors and dressed, then set off towards the river with a bundle of dirty clothes. The pink and orange had disappeared from the sky and the morning loomed grey and heavy. Lydia tried to lift her spirits again, but struggled to prevent a sense of despair settling over her. She was losing touch with her dreams. The sheer effort it took to get through one day after another was overwhelming. She hurried along the track, forcing herself on, until she reached the plateau of rocks from which the villagers – those who had no other means – plunged into the river to clean them- selves and their clothes. She was relieved that no one else was there so early. She left the clothes on a rock, walked to the river's edge and dropped carefully into the water.

It was cool and deliciously refreshing. Lydia swam slowly away from the bank, turning on to her back, then flipping over again, dolphin-like. She enjoyed the wash of the waves across her body. In that moment, she felt free to swim for ever. Free to leave her life behind and start a new one somewhere else, somewhere better. She floated effortlessly, gazing up at the sky and willing the sun to break through. But the clouds were too dense and there was no longer a breeze to brush them away. She rolled over on to her front and headed back to the bank. Joe and Kesi might wake and wonder where she was, and she hadn't started on the clothes yet.

As she scrambled up on to the rocks, she saw someone coming down the path towards her. It was Mandisa.

'Hey, Mandisa,' she called. 'How's your mama?'

Mandisa shrugged her shoulders. 'She needs to eat more. If she ate more she'd get better, but she says she's not hungry. How come you're here so early?'

'I'm starting work for Grandma Motsie so I need to get the chores done first.'

'Chores, how I hate chores. That's all I ever seem to do now. I wish Mama would get better so at least I wouldn't have to do so many chores any more,' Mandisa sighed. She sat down next to Lydia on the rocks.

Lydia smiled sadly. 'I'd do every single chore in the world if it would bring my mama back.'

'How will you like working for your grandmother?' Mandisa looked at her closely. 'Mama says she can be, well, difficult.'

'I'll have to put up with it. I don't have any choice.'

There was a long silence and then Mandisa said, so quietly that Lydia almost missed what she said, 'I don't know what I'll do if Mama dies.'

Lydia took hold of her friend's hand and squeezed it tight. She wanted to tell her that her mother wasn't going to die, but she couldn't. She wanted to tell her that everything would be all right, but she couldn't. 'I'll always be there for you,' she said as Mandisa's tears dropped on to her hand and she fought back her own. 'You only have to ask.'

Mandisa nodded, then pulled her hand away and stood up quickly. 'I don't know what's the matter with me,' she said. 'Mama's not going to die. It's not what you think it is. That's what bad people get. Mama's not bad. If I can just get her to eat more, that's all it is.' She ran to the river's edge and dived in.

When she re-emerged, Lydia stood up and shouted across at her, 'My mama wasn't bad, if that's what you think.'

But Mandisa had already dived again and resurfaced out of earshot. Lydia grabbed the pile of dirty clothes, gave them a brief scrub, then scrambled back up the path, almost tripping in her anxiety to get home.

Her brother and sister were still fast asleep when she went through the door. She roused them and told Joe to hurry and fetch the water. Kesi wanted her attention, but Lydia told her brusquely to dress ready for school, while she herself changed out of her wet clothes and set about preparing breakfast from the small amount of food that remained.

'As soon as Joe's back, I'll have to go,' she told Kesi. 'I won't have time to eat, so the two of you will have to eat on your own.'

'Where are you going?' Kesi asked.

'You know where,' Lydia replied. 'We talked about it last night. I'm going to work for Grandma.'

'What will you have to do?'

'I don't know, Kes, but you'll have to be a big grown-up girl and help Joe when I'm not here.'

'You'll be here when we come back from school, won't you? So I can read to you.'

'Of course I will,' said Lydia lightly, 'and if I work hard for Grandma, we won't have to go hungry any more and you'll be able to eat until you're as fat as a turkey.'

'I don't want to be as fat as a turkey,' Kesi pouted. 'Turkeys are ugly.'

'So are you when you pull a face like that. Look,

there's Joe. Be a good girl for him, and work hard in school.' Lydia gave her sister a hug, then went to meet Joe at the door. 'See you later, Joe,' she said, patting him on the shoulder, 'and thanks.'

Joe nodded, brushed past her to put the jug on the table, then turned and quietly asked, 'Are you sure you don't mind, Liddy? Working for Grandma, I mean, and not going to school?'

'If it makes our lives easier, then I don't mind,' she said. She walked off up the path before he could question her any further.

Chapter 9

Did I tell you how scared I am, Lydia? I am scared, so scared. You're asleep in your bed and I want so much to hold you tight like you're the grown-up and I'm the child. My hand is shaking as I write this. I'm scared not just for myself but for you and Joe and Kesi. How can I leave you? You are still so young, all of you. You need me. Children need their mother. And yet you will have to manage without me, and I will have to go on my journey alone.

I will be strong for you for as long as I can. I will try not to let you see or feel my fear. When you read these words I will be gone, but I want you to understand the pain it causes me to leave this life, and to leave you. I am telling you to keep yourself safe, Lydia, to keep your eyes wide open at all times so that you know when danger is heading your way. Do not give up your own life without a fight. It is too precious, even when it is so hard that all you want to do is curl up in a ball, close your eyes and shut it out.

Lydia gasped when she tapped on her grandmother's door and it was opened by Jabu Theki. He smiled broadly at her, a friendly smile, but she would rather he hadn't bothered.

'Mrs Motsie told me to expect you,' he said. 'She's taken to her bed with a fever, but says you're to get on with cleaning the house.'

'What are you doing here?' Lydia asked coldly.

'I'm working here. For the moment. Why are you always so hostile?'

'You're the one who called me Little Miss Snooty.'

'Jabu, is that Lydia?' The old lady's voice came from somewhere at the back of the house.

'Yes, Mrs Motsie,' Jabu replied. He winked conspiratorially at Lydia.

'Tell her to bring me a cup of coffee.'

'Yes, Mrs Motsie.'

'Why are you working here?' Lydia demanded.

'Because your grandmother asked me to. She says the place is falling apart and she wants it brought up to scratch so that she can spend her old age in comfort.'

'Why has she asked you to do it?'

'Because I'm the best.' Jabu grinned.

'Is that what you told her?'

'Lydia? What are you doing, girl? Am I to wait all day for you?' asked Grandma.

'You'd better leave the questions and boil the water before the old lady has apoplexy.' Jabu grinned again.

Lydia pushed past him, but realised that she didn't know if the kitchen was still in the same place. He pointed it out to her as she hesitated. She hurried towards it and pulled the door to behind her, but as she stared at the cupboards and tried to guess where the coffee was most likely to be, Jabu's face appeared at the window.

'Left side, back wall,' he said. 'Of course, if you really want to make this man happy, you'll make him coffee as well.'

'I don't, and I won't,' Lydia snapped. 'Now leave me alone, will you?'

Jabu put his hands in the air. 'Don't shoot an innocent man!' he squawked.

She picked up a wet cloth, but he had gone before she could throw it at him. She went to the cupboard he had indicated and opened it up. She was astonished at the amount of food she saw in front of her: tins of vegetables, packets of rice, jars of syrup. Up until that moment her hunger had been nothing more than a timid grumble. Now her stomach lurched with anticipation. Lydia quickly took hold of the packet of coffee, closed the cupboard door and searched for a pan. Another cupboard revealed a whole range of pans in different sizes. She grabbed the smallest and was about to search for a jug of water, when she remembered that Grandma Motsie had a kitchen tap. Hardly anyone in the village had a kitchen tap.

It was so much easier, wasn't it, Lydia, when we had hot and cold running water and lights that worked with the flick of a switch? We regained some things and lost others when we returned to the village. We were welcomed back with open arms. We rediscovered the closeness and the sense of belonging. This is where our ancestors roam. Our roots are here and they go such a long, long way down. But we lost those things that money and a good job and living in a town where life has moved forward can bring. When you leave the village again — and you must leave one day if you are to grow and flourish — don't sever your roots completely. They are a part of you. Without them you will lose something of who you are, and it may be your soul.

'Lydia! Must I dispense with your services before you have even begun? Where's my coffee? I could have gone to a plantation and picked the beans myself by now.'

'Coming, Grandma,' Lydia called from the door. She turned on the gas ring, set the pan of water to boil and searched the cupboards for a cup. When at last it was ready, she carried the cup carefully down the hallway and knocked on her grandmother's door.

She heard a testy 'Finally' from within, and opened the door slowly at the order, 'Come in, do.'

Her grandmother was sitting in bed, propped up against a pile of cushions. Lydia thought she looked perfectly well, though she was fanning herself and held her free hand to her neck. 'Put it here, and then stay while I give you your instructions.'

Lydia did as she was told, a fresh cloud of despair descending upon her as she stood in the cold of the old woman's glare.

'I shall treat you as a servant,' Grandma Motsie began. 'That way you will learn to know your place, and therefore be suitably trained for a career in service when you are old enough.'

'But –'

'Don't interrupt. To know your place means to listen when you are being spoken to. As well as looking after my personal needs, your duties will include cleaning the house and yard, running errands in the village and looking after the animals. I shall give you a list each day. When you have finished, you may return home. I shall expect you to be prompt at all times, unlike this morning, and to work hard. In return, I shall provide you with sufficient food, and I shall talk to the school as we discussed. You can begin by feeding the animals. Jabu – Mr Theki to you – will show you where everything is. And the house will need cleaning from top to bottom. I haven't been well enough to cope recently. Now, away with you, and leave me in peace.'

Lydia turned to go, but stopped when Grandma Motsie added, 'You will report to Mr Theki when I am not available, and you are to treat him with the same respect with which you treat me. And, Lydia, you will cook for him too.'

Lydia opened her mouth to say something, but realised it was pointless and returned to the kitchen. She stood by the window, looking out across her grandmother's land. Three cows were grazing in the furthest corner, where Jabu was at work repairing the fence. He had his shirt off and was whistling loudly. It was a song her father used to sing, out of tune, that was embedded in memories of happy days when he was still well and playing pranks on them.

He was such a prankster, your father. He would pretend to be gathered up in some task or other, absently singing away, detached from the rest of us, when suddenly you or Joe would let out a blood-curdling scream at the discovery of a cockroach amongst your underwear. We knew straight away who had put it there, but he carried on singing as though 'Innocence' was his middle name.

Lydia giggled at a sudden reckless desire to put a cockroach amongst Grandma Motsie's underwear, and then she wondered if her father had ever played such tricks on his mother. Would he have dared? She pondered on how very different her father had been from his mother. Where had his sense of fun, his carefree attitude come from? Not Grandma Motsie, that was certain, but not from his father either. It must have developed regardless of his parents. Could she rediscover the sense of fun she knew she had inherited from him, in spite of her grandmother and despite everything that had happened to her in the past few months? She hoped so. She didn't want to wind up bitter and twisted.

She stared out of the window again and caught her breath. It was as if she had set some magical force into play. One of her grandmother's goats was standing behind Jabu, who was bending over a piece of wood. She could see what the goat was about to do, and Jabu was completely unaware. The goat lowered its head and ran at him, connected with his bottom, pushing him face forward on to the ground, then began to eat his trousers. Lydia hooted with laughter. Jabu pulled himself to his feet, shooed the goat away and looked towards the house. Lydia drew back from the window, hoping he hadn't seen her, then exploded with laughter again.

Baba would have loved that, she thought. *Baba would have engineered that!*

She pulled herself together and picked up the list that had been left for her on the table. It was a long list. Was she really expected to do all those things in one day? Lydia was sure Grandma Motsie had put down every job she could think of, just for the sake of it. Well, she wasn't going to be beaten by it. She would start from the top and work her way through it, carefully, methodically, and if there wasn't time to complete everything before she had to leave to take care of Joe and Kesi, she would apologise and promise to reach the end the next day. The old woman wouldn't be able to keep inventing tasks.

Chapter 10

Lydia was wrong. So wrong. Grandma Motsie's capacity for invention was extraordinary, and devastating.

Over the next two weeks, Lydia wasn't allowed to stop. Her grandmother spent the first two days in bed but made continuous demands. She would call out, expecting Lydia to drop what she was doing and come running. Her water glass was empty, the sheets on the bed needed tucking in, she had dropped her magazine, there was a mosquito annoying her, she was too cold, she was too hot, there was a spider on the floor, she wanted some fruit, she wanted the shutters opened, she wanted the shutters closed. Lydia was convinced that as soon as she went out of the room, her grandmother tiptoed over to the door and listened to what she was doing, because the minute she set about a new task she was interrupted.

Dealing with Grandma Motsie's personal needs was only a small part of what was expected of her. There were constant errands to be carried out, and no sooner had she returned from one than another one arose. She would come all the way back from the village with a basket full of vegetables, only to be sent back again to fetch a bag of lemons. She would be asked to collect some painkillers from the clinic, then, on her return, told to take a message to someone who lived two doors from the clinic. It wouldn't have been so bad if there weren't all the household chores to be done as well. In fact, Lydia preferred to be away from the house, where she couldn't be nagged and scolded.

The chores were endless. The kitchen floor had to be mopped three times a day. The kitchen itself had to be kept spotless, and once Grandma Motsie was back on her feet she checked it regularly. At the slightest trace of a grease mark or a crumb, everything had to be scrubbed down again. There was always washing to be done. Lydia believed her grandmother was deliberately making things dirty when the same items reappeared several days in a row. At least she could do it in the sink, rather than going down to the river, but when she mixed colours with whites in hot water and turned a pile of white underwear grey, her grandmother halved her food allowance to pay for replacements. The yard outside had to be swept daily, the chickens had to be fed morning and evening, wood had to be collected for the fires, the water barrel had to be topped up, and then there were meals to be made. Lydia had learned to cook with her mother; simple, nourishing meals. But it had been a long time since she had had the ingredients available to do anything more than make porridge or a stew. And she had never cooked on a stove like Grandma Motsie's, which seemed to burn things when she took her eyes off them even for a moment. The old woman would often stand behind her, delivering instructions, which turned Lydia's fingers into thumbs.

The worst thing was that it was always dark before she was able to leave at the end of the day. She begged to be allowed to go earlier, but her grandmother insisted that she stay until she had finished everything on the list. It was only then that she would allow Lydia to take a parcel of food away with her to feed Joe and Kesi.

By the time Lydia arrived home, Joe was grumpy and tired from babysitting Kesi, and Kesi was tearful because she was hungry and wanted attention. On the days when Joe had football training after school, Kesi had to stay at school as well. Lydia tried, on her one day off, to arrange with other parents for Kesi to go home with them when Joe had to stay late, but so many of them were looking after additional children already. Others refused without giving a reason. Lydia was shocked when she realised how many children in the village had lost one or both parents. Grandparents like Grandma Motsie were bringing up their grand-children and most were very poor. Grandma Motsie was lucky. Grandpa Motsie had had a good job and had left her well provided for.

'When you've put up with what I've put up with, you deserve a little comfort in your old age,' she said more than once. 'Not that that means I have money to fritter away.'

And then there was Jabu. He was always there, smiling, talking to her, ignoring her sullen responses, acting as though they were the best of friends. Lydia did as she was told, took him drinks and provided him with meals, but she refused to answer his probing questions about her life. Sometimes he made her smile to herself with his antics – he was very good at mimicking her grandmother and other villagers – but she would never let him see that, in case he took advantage and tried to get closer to her. He worked hard, she thought, and her grandmother treated him well. Very well. Better than she did her own family.

One day, Grandma Motsie called her into her room and, quite unaccountably, began to talk to her about Jabu.

'That's a good man,' she said, pointing at him through the window. 'A fine man, Jabu Theki. A woman could do far worse than to settle down with a man like that, don't you think, Lydia?'

Lydia was so embarrassed she didn't know what to say. The last thing she wanted to do was to discuss men with her grandmother and she certainly didn't want to discuss Jabu with her, especially since he had a habit of appearing in her life whichever direction she took. The thought that Grandma might one day insist that she marry him made her shiver inwardly.

'Speak up, girl,' the old woman said. 'It's something you'll have to give thought to yourself one day.'

'I don't ever want to get married,' Lydia said at last. 'I want to study hard and get a good job and make sure Joe and Kesi are happy.'

'Don't talk such nonsense. Of course you'll get married. Girls like you don't get good jobs. You'll need a man to look after you if you don't want to spend the rest of your life starving. And it's your duty to our village to marry and have babies.'

What about my duty to myself? Lydia wanted to argue.

She didn't, though, because she knew there was no point.

'There are plenty of good men, like your father and your grandfather,' Grandma Motsie persisted.

But my father – your son – wasn't always a good man, thought Lydia. *Not when it mattered. Not when it really mattered. He let us down. He let us all down. Like so many other fathers. I don't want that. I don't want to be let down, because that would mean that I'm letting my children down.*

'You can't afford to keep aloof, young lady. Not when a good man crosses your path.'

'When that time comes, perhaps I will change my mind, Grandma.'

'Pah, by the time you pull your head out of the clouds, you'll be too old for any man to pay you attention.'

Lydia didn't answer and was glad that her grandmother sent her about her work straight afterwards. She attacked the rest of the tasks on her list with as much speed as she could muster, hoping that she wouldn't see Jabu again that day. She couldn't face him, not after what her grandmother had said. Luckily, he seemed to have disappeared for the afternoon, but at the end of the day she kept her head down as she hurried away from the house, just in case he was lurking somewhere.

Kesi was more tearful than ever when she arrived home. She had been pushed over at school. On seeing her bloody knees, the other children had run off and left her.

'The boys and girls don't like me, Liddy,' she wailed. 'They think I'm bad in the middle.'

'It's only because people tell them silly things, Kes,' Lydia hushed, lifting her on to her lap. She was glad to discover that her sister felt a little heavier and less bony, thanks to the food Grandma Motsie spared for them. It wasn't much, but it was more than they had been able to scrape together without her help. 'You're not bad in the middle and you're not bad on the outside. In fact, you're so delicious all the way through that I'm going to eat you all up.' She took hold of one of Kesi's fingers and pretended to eat it.

'Tickles,' Kesi giggled and sniffed at the same time.

'That's better,' said Lydia. 'Now, let me have a proper look at those knees.'

'Mrs Buthelezi cleaned them up and said I was brave.'

'She wants to see you tomorrow,' Joe said abruptly. He had been sitting on the bed staring into space while Lydia dealt with Kesi.

'Why does she want to see me?'

'I don't know, do I? She just said to ask you to go in.'

'Don't be grumpy, Joe. I'm doing my best.'

'You haven't had to listen to Kes crying her eyes out for the last hour.'

'No, but I've had Grandma going on at me.'

'You should tell her to go and hang herself.'

'Joe! Don't say things like that.'

'Well, it was better before. It was better when you were here, even if we didn't have much to eat. You're never here any more when we need you.'

He sounded so fed up, Lydia began to think that perhaps she wasn't doing the right thing. A small fluttering of her heart confirmed what she knew already – that she would rejoice if she didn't have to go back to work for her grandmother. But the tiny arms that were wrapped round her waist reminded her that they had barely survived when they were on their own. It would be even worse now. She had been unable to spend any time in the garden since working for Grandma Motsie, and it was now completely overrun with weeds.

'The most important thing is school. If I don't do as Grandma wants, there'll be no more school, no more football and no more parcels of food. And I don't know how I'm supposed to go and see Mrs Buthelezi to-morrow when I have to be at work.'

Joe stretched out lengthways on the bed. The light from an oil lamp played across his face. His eyes were closed, his hands clasped tightly together.

It's not his problem, Lydia thought to herself. *It shouldn't be his problem.*

She lifted Kesi on to the floor so that she could begin preparing their meal. There was no water. The meal needed water.

'Did you forget the water, Joe?' Lydia asked quietly.

'How could I get water when I had Kes blubbering? I missed my football training because of Kes, and all she wanted was you.' He rolled over on to his side so that his back was towards her.

'I'm sorry about the football training. Do you want to stay here with Kes while I fetch it, or do you want to go while I stay?' Lydia hardly dared speak the words, she was so nervous of Joe's reaction.

He lay still, without responding.

'Joe?'

She went over and gently touched his foot. He shot up

from the bed, grabbed the water jug and burst out of the rondavel. Lydia wanted to cry.

Kesi took hold of her hand. 'Joe's always cross with me too,' she whispered.

'He's not unkind, is he?' Lydia hated asking such a question.

'Only cross. I think he doesn't want to look after me any more.'

Lydia squeezed her hand. 'We can't blame him for being cross about missing his football. He'll be all right again tomorrow.'

'He says he wishes he could run away and be on his own and join a football team and never have to do any schoolwork again.'

Lydia felt a stab of guilt. She hadn't been able to help Joe with his maths for so long. It was too late by the time they had eaten, and it was difficult to see properly once the daylight had faded.

'I'll talk to him when he comes back. Let's get these potatoes peeled.'

'When will you listen to me read again?' Kesi asked when they had finished.

'On my next day off, and I promise to help you with your maths as well,' she said to Joe, who had just returned.

He grunted in reply. For the rest of the evening, he spoke only when she addressed him, even when she suggested that he should ask Mrs Buthelezi to send her a letter.

Lydia lay awake that night, the events of the day tumbling over and over in her mind. Life seemed to be closing in on her again and this time she couldn't see her way forward. She lit a candle and picked up her mother's book.

The night-time is the worst, Lydia, when we can't sleep. It should feel cosy and safe when the dark wraps itself round us like a thick blanket. Instead, it brings demons with it. When we're awake in the night, our senses leap to red alert. Our ears pick up every tiny unusual sound. Our noses can sniff out the slightest odd smell. Yet our eyes, straining to detect any foreign form through the dense blackness, are robbed of their ability to see. And so our minds turn in on themselves and create images that feed our fears. I pray for sleep to carry me away to my dreams, yet in the deep of the night I'm scared that it will refuse to bring me back, and so I fight it. I pray for the dawn to announce the coming of a new day and to tell me that I have survived another night. It is then that I stop fighting and allow sleep to take over.

I wish for you that the night will be your friend and not your enemy, Lydia. I wish that sleep will rock you in its arms and hold you safe, until you are ready to wake and embrace another beautiful day.

A strange warmth spread itself around Lydia's waist and hips. Kesi had wet the bed again.

Chapter 11

Kesi began to wet the bed again regularly. Lydia tried to stay awake so that she could take her sister to the toilet midway through the night, but mostly she was too tired. It meant that when she got up in the morning to do the chores, she had to disturb Joe and Kesi as well, strip the sheet from the bed and take it down to the river. She left for work with the sheet flapping in the garden like some public announcement of her family's troubles. Sometimes it was still there when she arrived home in the evening – when Joe had either forgotten to bring it in, or refused to because he was too fed up with waking soaked to want anything more to do with the consequences.

Lydia became increasingly worried about Joe. He had changed so much. He was grumpier than ever, but wouldn't allow her to draw him into conversation. As soon as she arrived home, he took himself outside, sat against the wall and rolled a ball from side to side under the arch of his legs. Or he lay down on the bed and didn't budge until she had set their meal on the table. During the meal, he answered her questions in mono-syllables, never smiling if she made a joke and grunting when she asked how his schoolwork was going.

Meanwhile, Kesi was so distressed about wetting the bed that she was tearful from the moment she woke up. She started refusing to drink and then began to eat less and less, because she thought that way she wouldn't be able to wee, however much Lydia cajoled her and told her it wasn't the answer. She sobbed when Lydia had to leave for work, promising every day that she wouldn't wet the bed that night.

Lydia tried to explain the situation to Grandma Motsie but, as she expected, the old woman didn't want to know.

'Your sister has been trouble from the day she was born,' she said. 'Mollycoddling her now isn't going to help her. She must learn to cope with things like the rest of us.'

'But if I could just go home early enough to be there for them when they get back from school,' Lydia pleaded.

'Do you think, when you are in employment, that you will be allowed to disappear off home whenever you feel like it?'

'But this is different, Grandma. Kesi needs me at the moment and it's very hard for Joe to look after her.'

'I have had my say on the subject. If your brother and sister want to eat and go to school, then you must earn it for them. Nothing comes easily in this world, and they had better learn that sooner rather than later. They are lucky to have me to provide for them. Now, get on with your work, please, Lydia.'

As her grandmother waved her away, Lydia caught sight of Jabu hovering behind the door, cap in hand, waiting to come in. She wondered how much he had heard. What did he think of Grandma Motsie for the way she treated her family? He touched her on the arm as she went past him.

'You keep fighting there, little one,' he whispered.

She looked into his face and he winked. She couldn't tell if he was being genuinely supportive or mocking her. At that moment, she didn't care. She desperately wanted some time on her own to decide what she should do. The days were merging into one another, a treadmill of endless chores, endless demands, endless worry. She had solved one crisis, but created another that threatened to overwhelm her. At the same time, boiling up inside her was a hatred for her grandmother that she could scarcely control any longer. She contained it by focusing on the parcels of food she took home at the end of each day and the knowledge that Joe and Kesi were going to school. But at what cost to their happiness did she disappear at dawn? At what cost to her own happiness? Was there another way? Did she have any choice?

You will know that you are truly rich when you can make choices in your life. I could make choices once upon a time, real choices, choices that led to happiness and laughter and a sense of being fulfilled. When I became ill, all but the smallest of choices were taken away from me, and from you, poor child. But you will have choices again. Real choices. Choices that will leave you at peace with yourself and with the world. Our country is changing fast. There will be so many more opportunities for people like us to spread our wings. Make the right choices when they come, Lydia, and they will come. Keep reaching out, keep believing in yourself and one day you will make choices that will allow you to fly.

Having a real choice meant being offered an option that was better than another one, didn't it? Lydia thought.

Or having more than one option, both of which would be equally agreeable. It wasn't just a question of choosing the lesser of two evils. That wasn't choice. That was like being trapped somewhere and facing death whichever way out you took – straight into a lion's mouth one way, straight over the edge of a mountain the other. That's where she was right now, and she couldn't see that she would ever be in the position to make any real choices. Her grandmother was grooming her for a life of servitude. What choices would she have if she were made to follow that route? Real choices were things like deciding where to live, whether or not to marry, who to marry, what sort of career to pursue, what sort of food to eat, how much food to eat. Having a real choice meant being able to decide your own future, not having it mapped out by someone else, especially someone with a heart as cold as ice.

'Daydreaming as usual, Lydia? And there you were, asking to go home early.'

Her grandmother's rasping voice jolted her from her thoughts. The old woman's short round frame filled the doorway. Behind her, Jabu, head and shoulders taller, was pulling funny faces.

'I'm going out for a while and leaving Jabu in charge. You will do as he says – is that understood?'

Jabu wagged his finger above Grandma Motsie's head.

Lydia stifled a giggle and for a moment was unable to speak. She gave a slight nod, but it wasn't enough for Grandma Motsie, who insisted that she find her tongue. Jabu rolled his eyes inwards and back again, then stuck out his tongue.

'Yes, Grandma,' Lydia managed to splutter.

She ignored the tutting that followed, together with the loud complaints about her that were aimed in Jabu's direction, and began to prepare her grandmother's evening meal. She was grateful to Jabu for giving her a reason to smile, but it didn't change how she felt about the situation she was in, and as she scrubbed at a particularly dirty potato a sombre despair engulfed her. She stood at the sink, fully expecting that Jabu would use the opportunity of his employer's absence to play the big boss himself, however much he might have larked around a few minutes before. He didn't though. He went straight out into the garden and spent the rest of the afternoon hoeing between the rows of vegetables. He stopped and asked how she was getting on when she took him a drink, but otherwise left her alone.

Lydia was glad. She didn't want to talk to anyone. She didn't want anyone to come near her. She didn't even want to go home, because she couldn't bear another evening with Kesi clinging to her and Joe's sullenness. She could feel herself resenting more and more the role that had been thrust upon her. She was doing her best, but nobody else seemed to be trying, nobody else gave a thought to how she felt. The pain of losing her mother was stronger now than ever. It was so intense it was like a physical hurt, like someone kicking her over and over again. She wanted her mother back. She wanted her arms round her. She wanted to hear her voice telling her everything was all right and there was nothing for her to worry about. She wiped a tear angrily from her cheek.

'Why did you have to leave us, Mama?' she whispered. 'Couldn't you have tried harder to stay, at least until I was old enough?'

I have fought so long and hard, Lydia. I believed that if I kept strong in my head and my heart, I could force my body to build a wall against the tyranny of this illness. I have failed. I look at my hands as I write these words and I don't recognise them. They are the hands of a woman twice my age, and they shake like fragile leaves in a breeze. My head tells me to jump up from this bed, to gather my children to me and run with them into the wind, shouting for joy that we have life and will live it. But my body won't respond. I look at you sitting next to me, pretty in your thoughts, and I no longer have the strength to reach out to you.

Just before darkness fell, she heard Jabu wiping his boots outside the front door and the clatter as he dropped them on to the ground. She tried to pull herself together. He padded into the kitchen in his bare feet, crossing to the sink to wash his hands.

'Your grandmother treats you very badly,' he said, without turning round.

Lydia stopped what she was doing.

'She would treat a stray dog better, yet you're her family. Why, Lydia? Why is that?'

He was looking at her now. She turned her head away from him, not knowing what to say.

'Don't you trust me, Lydia? Do I look like I can't be trusted?'

Lydia glanced at him quickly, then stared at the ground again.

'Shall I tell you how you look? You look like the sweetest girl I have ever seen. Your face is so pretty. You look sad, though. Why wouldn't you, when your life is so hard? Your eyes are crying out for help. I can help you, Lydia. I can help you, and I can help your brother and your little sister. I have money. I have money to send them to school, to buy you shoes and clothes, to take you away from the misery of being your grandmother's slave. I want to hold you in my arms and push the sadness away. I want to make you laugh again.'

I want you to remember how it feels to laugh and laugh until your ribs are about to burst.

'I want to protect you. Can I be your protector, Lydia?' He laid his arm on her shoulder.

Beware of men, Lydia.

'I will take care of you, Lydia. I will look after you,' he whispered.

There are those who will see a vulnerable girl before them and offer their protection. It's not protection they are offering, you know that, don't you?

She pushed him back, wriggling to free herself from his grasp.

'Leave me alone,' she cried. 'Get away from me, leave me alone.'

He caught hold of her wrists as she tried to beat him. 'Steady,' he smirked. 'You don't want me to have you arrested for assault.'

'Just let me go.' Lydia was sobbing now.

'I'll let you go.' His voice was mocking again. 'You're just a kid. What would I want with a kid?' He let go with a short laugh and Lydia nearly lost her balance as she pulled away.

She rushed to the door, then turned back and hissed, 'My mother warned me about men like you.'

'Your mother did, did she?' he taunted. 'But your mother didn't care enough about you not to go and get sick, did she?'

'She died of AIDS. Why don't you say it? She died of AIDS and it wasn't her fault,' Lydia screamed it at him. 'It's your fault, men like you who just use people then spit them out.'

'That's not a nice thing to say about your father.' He grinned at her.

Lydia wanted to hit him, to wipe the taunting smile from his face. She picked up one of her grandmother's pots and hurled it across the room at him. Then she turned and fled, running blindly down the dusty road, terrified that he might come after her.

Chapter 12

Lydia's heart was still pounding when, finally, she came to the path that led to her home. She stared back up the road, relieved to see that there was still no sign of Jabu. She wasn't ready to go inside, and Joe and Kesi wouldn't be expecting her yet. She continued towards the river instead, keeping to the shadows to avoid being seen. It was nearly dark. A few people were tidying up outside their rondavels, or sitting in the last light of the sun, gazing into space. Lydia felt like a wild animal hunting for prey as she crept soundlessly along the edge of the path. She had just one intention: to wash away every last trace of her encounter with Jabu.

When she reached the river, she checked that nobody else was about, then slipped slowly into the water. She swam away from the bank, moving faster and faster, until she was knifing through the current. As soon as she reached the middle, she plunged under the water, forcing herself downwards, downwards, until she was satisfied that she was clean. With her lungs bursting, she shot up to the surface again, wiped her hands over her face, then lay on her back, staring up at the blackening sky.

'What have I done, Mama?' she murmured. 'What's going to happen now?'

Lydia trawled her memory for her mother's words, words she had read so often, words that might help her to find a way forward, but they kept escaping or jumbling themselves together so that they made no sense. She turned over on to her front again and began to swim slowly towards the shore, where she scrambled up the bank and made her way back up the path in the half-light. She pulled the sheet from the line, took a deep breath and went inside.

'Liddy, Liddy, Liddy!' Kesi shouted happily.

'You're early,' said Joe, without looking up.

'I'm not going back,' Lydia announced brightly.

'What do you mean, you're not going back?' This time, Joe gave Lydia his full attention.

'I'm not going to work for Grandma any more.'

She watched as her brother's face changed from astonished, to pleased, to concerned.

'Has something happened?' he asked.

'I just decided that I need to be here more.'

'Kes and I can manage,' Joe said gruffly.

'No, you can't,' said Lydia quickly, adding, 'you shouldn't have to. It's not fair. Anyway, I don't think Grandma will want me to work for her any more.'

'Course she will,' scoffed Joe. 'No one else will work for her on what she gives us.'

'Not when she finds out I broke one of her pots, she won't.'

'What are you talking about, Liddy?' Joe was beginning to sound exasperated. 'She won't get rid of you over a broken pot.'

'I'm not going back, Joe, and that's final,' Lydia snapped. 'We'll have to manage on our own from now on.'

She started to put the sheet on the bed, flattening it so savagely that a tear appeared across the middle. Kesi giggled nervously, stopping the minute Lydia glared at her. Lydia tried to control the turmoil of feelings that were beseiging her, but she couldn't. She sat on the bed and broke down in tears. Joe and Kesi stood watching her, both too shocked to move, then sat on either side and put their arms round her.

'Don't worry, Liddy,' Joe said at last. 'We'll be all right.'

'We haven't even got anything to eat tonight,' Lydia sobbed.

'We haven't eaten plenty of times before,' said Joe.

'I'm not hungry,' added Kesi.

'But what about tomorrow and the next day and the next?'

'If we work really hard in the garden we can get it going again.' Joe sounded so sure.

'We tried before and it didn't work,' said Lydia.

'Then we'll have to try harder,' said Joe. 'Perhaps you could give that Mr Theki another chance.'

'No!' Lydia stood up abruptly, pushing her brother and sister away. 'Never. I don't want you ever to mention his name again.'

'Why? What's he done that's so bad?'

'It doesn't matter what he's done, just do as I say.'

There was a silence again, broken only by Kesi's foot tapping anxiously on the leg of the bed.

'I'm sorry,' said Lydia at last. 'I didn't mean to shout. And I didn't mean to make things even more difficult for us.'

'There'll be one thing that's better,' said Kesi. 'You'll be here when we come home from school.'

'I forgot,' Joe butted in. 'There's a letter for you

from school. Mrs Buthelezi asked me to make sure you got it.'

Lydia took the letter and opened it. She read it, folded it up again and put it down. Her brother and sister waited for her to say something, but she went outside and stared through the dark at the garden. When she hadn't come back in after a few moments, Joe went to find her.

'What does the letter say, Liddy?'

Lydia tugged at a weed that came up to her waist. 'It says that the school fees haven't been paid. They want to know what arrangements are being made. They say that in case of hardship we could qualify for a grant.'

'But Grandma was supposed to go and see them. She was supposed to tell them we couldn't pay. She was supposed to deal with all that. That's what you told me, Liddy.'

'She hasn't done it.'

'You mean she couldn't even do that for us? That's the only reason you were working for her. You're not going back, Lid, even if you change your mind. I won't let you. You're never going back, OK?'

Lydia put her hand on Joe's shoulder. 'I wouldn't go back if she paid me real money,' she said, managing to smile. 'I'll go to the school and deal with it myself, and I don't care if it upsets Grandma or not.'

'I'll come with you if you like,' said Joe. 'We're in this together, Liddy, and we're going to be fine.'

They went back inside. Lydia found a shrivelled sweet potato that had fallen under the table, the tops from two carrots and a few grains of rice at the bottom of a packet. She boiled them together and served up a watery soup. Nobody complained. Joe said that when the weekend came he would dig the garden until his hands blistered. Kesi said she would bring her lunch home from school so that Lydia could share it. Lydia was determined that she would find some sort of work that would mean she could be at home when they came back from school.

It all seemed so simple when they sat around the table that evening making their plans. They would all muck in together and somehow everything would be all right. In the deep dark of the night, however, as Lydia lay wide awake listening to the cicadas, nothing could have seemed less simple. She was scared, not just of the difficulties they faced, but of her grandmother. What would Jabu have said to her? How would Grandma Motsie react? What harm could she do to them?

'What did Jabu do that makes you hate him so much?' Joe's voice whispered, soft, urgent.

'I don't trust him, that's all. He gives me the creeps. And he was saying things about Mama.'

'I'll kill him.'

'No, you won't. You're not to go near him.'

'But I promised Mama I'd look after you when I'm older. I'm older now and he deserves a beating.'

'He deserves to be ignored and you're no good to us in prison.'

Joe grunted in response. Just when Lydia thought he had gone back to sleep, he said, 'I miss Mama. And Baba. I miss them so much it hurts sometimes.'

'I miss them too, all the time.'

'Sometimes I can't see their faces any more. Sometimes I can't hear their voices either. I'm scared when that happens they'll disappear for ever.'

'We're lucky we have photos. At least we can look at those to remind us. Mama said that when Baba came home with a camera, she wanted to shoot him. He'd spent most of his wages on it. Mama was so cross, but he was so happy. She said he wanted to take pictures of everything and everyone, but she wouldn't let him because there were only twenty-four frames and he wasn't going to be able to buy another film.'

'What happened to the camera?'
'Somebody stole it.'

They stole the television too, Lydia, can you believe that? They were the first things we had bought that told us we were really beginnning to throw off the noose of poverty. Your father had a good job, I was working too and we were ready to fly. That was a cruel blow. It was like somebody saying to us: 'You have no right to do that. You must stay where you are, flying is not for the likes of you.' Your father, he scoured the streets looking for someone carrying his camera. I said to him, 'How are you going to know it's your camera?' 'I'll know,' he said. But he never did catch anyone, and he never did buy another camera. You see, it wasn't just the camera those people stole. It was a little bit of your father's hope for the future.

'Some people say only bad people get AIDS,' Joe interrupted Lydia's thoughts. 'They say it's God's punishment because they've offended him.'

'You know that's not true.'

'But then why do good people get AIDS?'

It was a question Lydia had asked herself. 'Perhaps it's because good people can be led astray by bad people. And because bad people have the power to bring good people down,' she said.

'Like Grandma's trying to bring us down?'

'I don't know, Joe. I don't know why things are the way they are. I don't know why Grandma Motsie is like she is. She's not going to bring us down, though.'

'We won't let her, will we, Liddy?'

Chapter 13

The next morning dawned wet and colder than it had been for some time. Lydia stood in the doorway and watched the rain pooling in the yard. It was a good beginning if they were to sort the garden out. A few days of rain would soften the ground and make it easier to dig. She resolved to see if she could borrow a spade from Mandisa's family. She resolved too that she would learn how to make clay pots so that she could sell them at market along with the vegetables they grew. She wondered if she could earn a bit of money working for someone in the village, just to have enough to buy some seeds. She would go to the school first though. She would go and wait outside the Head's office, not like a child who had done something wrong, but because she had the role of a grown-up now, the role of head of the family.

You may have to become someone else to survive, Lydia.

As Joe and Kesi stirred in the bed, the doubts came creeping back. There was nothing to eat that morning, and it would be some time before the garden would produce anything worthwhile. She had no idea what sort of reception she would be given at the school. She was certain that at some stage her grandmother would appear, and she was scared that Jabu would continue to taunt her. Perhaps the best thing would be for them to leave the village and find a new home in one of the nearby townships. It would be easier for her to earn money there, she thought, and no one would be aware of their background. People had become such strangers to them in their own village; it wouldn't really make much difference if they moved somewhere where they didn't know anybody. Even so, the idea of leaving behind everything they knew was terrifying.

Lydia began to busy herself to take her mind off such worries. She put on her best clothes, which she was startled to discover were becoming too small for her — she must have grown without realising it.

By the time her brother and sister woke up, she was

ready to get going and chivvied them along in her anxiety not to lose her nerve. They stepped out into the rain and hurried through the village, joining the groups of other children who were also on their way to school. Some of them looked at her curiously because she wasn't in uniform and because they hadn't seen her making the trip to school in a long while. Some – friends of Joe – tagged along with them, chattering loudly about football. Lydia tried to block out their voices so that she could rehearse what she wanted to say to Mrs Dlamini. When they went through the school-gates, several pupils from Lydia's class asked if she would be coming back. She shook her head. Sophie and one of her other friends promised they would visit her at home, but Lydia knew they wouldn't. Their lives had moved on, and so had hers.

Let me tell you about friends. Everyone needs friends, Lydia. True friends are those who are there for you when you need them. True friends laugh with you and cry with you. True friends don't judge you, they accept you as you are and love you for who you are. True friends are loyal and worthy of your trust. Be a true friend, Lydia, and you will find true friends yourself.

Events take over sometimes, Mama, thought Lydia. *Events take over, and it doesn't matter how much you mean to do something, you fail because everything changes and suddenly you don't know where you are any more. You don't even know who you are any more. And how can I stay friends with children who talk about their mothers, when it makes me sad to listen to them?*

Lydia waved goodbye to Joe and Kesi and walked along the corridor to the Head's office. All over the walls were pictures that pupils had painted. Lydia was amazed to see that one of them was by Joe. It was good, very good.

When had that talent developed, she wondered, *and why didn't I realise it was there?*

But, of course, without paper and paints at home for Joe to express himself with, how could she know? As she stood and waited, she heard the school song. She mouthed the words and wished again that she could be part of this world where grown-ups made decisions for you.

How can I stay friends with children who are still in their childhood, when I have all the responsibilities of a grown-up? she asked herself. *I'm even thinking like a grown-up now!*

The door to the Head's office opened. 'Lydia, dear, what a nice surprise.' Mrs Dlamini smiled.

Lydia allowed herself to be ushered inside, but was increasingly anxious about what she was going to say.

Mrs Dlamini began by asking how she was getting on, and expressed her regrets that Lydia was not continuing her education. 'Is there anything that can be done about that?'

Lydia shrugged. 'I came to see you about the fees. We don't have the money to pay for Joe and Kesi. I told Mama I would make sure they stayed in school, but there's no money left.'

'I understood that your grandmother was taking care of you. Is that not the case?'

Lydia kept her eyes averted. 'She doesn't have the money either.'

Mrs Dlamini looked at her curiously. 'And she sent you to see me?'

'I don't think she wants to come.'

'Would you like us to talk to her?'

'No,' Lydia said quickly. 'She's very proud.' Then she added, 'I don't think she likes us very much. It might make things worse.'

'If she's your guardian, Lydia, then we need to speak with her.'

'She's not. Not any more. Not now.'

There was silence as Mrs Dlamini took in what Lydia had said. Lydia shifted uncomfortably on her chair under the Head's intense scrutiny.

'So you're managing all on your own?' Mrs Dlamini said at last.

Lydia nodded weakly.

'I'll see what I can do for you, Lydia. You're not the only children in the school who are struggling – not by any means. There's nothing to feel ashamed about, though I appreciate that not everyone views it that way.'

'Thank you, Mrs Dlamini.'

'In the meantime, Joe and Kesi should continue to come in as usual – and I hope we can find some way for you to return.'

'There's always so much to do,' Lydia replied.

'I know, child, I know.'

Mrs Dlamini closed their meeting by recommending that Lydia apply for a government grant to help with food and other essential items.

'Can I do that?' Lydia was amazed.

'You'll have to go into the town to collect the forms, and it may take some time, but, yes, you can do that.'

Lydia felt as if a great weight had been lifted from her shoulders. She wanted to skip down the corridor, especially when she heard laughter coming from one of the classrooms.

'You've made a start,' she said to herself.

It had stopped raining when she stepped out of the schoolgates and began the steep trek up the hill to Mandisa's homestead. She hadn't been to visit since long before her mother had died, though Mandisa had called by to see her. She planned to make up for it now and help her friend in whatever way she could, despite what Mandisa had said the last time they met.

But when she reached the plateau where Mandisa's family's homestead nestled amongst a group of others, Lydia saw that something wasn't right. Villagers were clustered outside the rondavel and she could hear chanting coming from inside. She knew instantly what was happening: it had been the same when both of her parents had died. The neighbours were there because of a family bereavement.

Poor Mandisa, she thought.

Lydia hurried back down the path before she could be swept up in the haunting expressions of grief that were being carried towards her by the wind. She had no place at such a gathering. She would have to wait to see her friend, and then she would be a true friend to her.

Chapter 14

When Lydia walked down the path and turned into her home, she saw her grandmother sitting on a chair outside. Her first instinct was to run away, but Grandma Motsie had already spotted her, and she had to face her sooner or later.

'Ah, there you are, Lydia,' the old woman said. 'Tell me, what day of the week is it?'

'I think you know, Grandma,' Lydia murmured.

'And where have you been?'

Lydia didn't answer.

'Where should you have been?'

Lydia didn't answer again.

'Shall I tell you where you should have been and what you should have been doing?'

'I'm not doing it any more,' Lydia said quietly.

There was a moment's pause, before Grandma Motsie continued, as if she hadn't heard. 'I'll help you, Lydia, shall I? Apart from the fact that you are in my employ and I didn't give you permission to take a day's leave, there is the small matter of a broken pot. A pot which Jabu says you broke accidentally, but a pot which nevertheless has to be paid for. Do you have the money to pay for it, Lydia?'

Lydia shook her head dully.

'Then you will have to pay for it by working extra hours for me.' She fixed Lydia with a triumphant glare.

Lydia could have withered under that glare, like she had done so many times before. Instead, a huge wave of anger swept up through her, fuelled by the injustice she felt at the situation she found herself in. 'I'm not going to work for you any more, Grandma,' she said simply. 'It wasn't what Mama would have wanted.' She took a deep breath and added, 'I don't think it's what Baba would have wanted either.'

The words hung in the air, until the full force of them rocked Grandma Motsie in her chair. 'How dare you tell me what my son would have wanted.' She hauled herself awkwardly to her feet. 'He didn't know what he wanted himself once he fell under your mother's spell. And then look what she did to him.'

'Mama did nothing to him. He did it to himself,' Lydia cried. She didn't care now if she was being disrespectful. She didn't care what her grandmother thought. 'He caught AIDS because he was unfaithful to Mama and then he gave it to her as well. I hate him for that.'

'Lies, it's all lies. That's just what your mother told you to cover up her own guilt.'

'What guilt? All she did was try to be a good wife and a good mother.'

'Her guilt at being a witch. It's a pity she wasn't punished for that before she poisoned your poor father.'

Lydia was astonished at the venom with which the old woman abused her mother. She wanted to lash out at her to make her stop. She wanted her to go away. 'My mother was an angel,' she said finally.

'Ha! And she's filled your head with nonsense. I know. I've been reading it while I've been waiting for you to come back. All that rubbish about following your dreams and making something of yourself. Hardly practical, is it? Hardly how to cook a meal, or how to keep a clean home, or how to keep a man happy, is it?'

'You had no right!' Lydia hurled at her.

'I'm your guardian. I have every right,' Grandma Motsie flung back at her.

'You're not my guardian, not any more. We can manage on our own.'

'You'll soon come back when you haven't any food in your belly and when they throw Joe and that precious sister of yours out of school.'

'I won't, Grandma, and I'd like you to leave now.'

'You think you can get rid of me just like that? I'll leave now because I choose to, but you haven't heard the last of this.'

She pushed past Lydia and waddled up the path to the road. A truck was waiting there. It took Lydia a moment to realise that the driver was Jabu. She watched him get out to help her grandmother inside, then as soon as they had gone she ran indoors. She went straight to her mother's memory box and took out her book. Even the thought that her grandmother had handled it made her feel sick. She opened it carefully, running her hand over each sheet of paper, her mother's words dancing in front of her, until she came to a torn page. Half of it had been ripped out. And then she found another torn page, and another. What was missing? It didn't take her long to remember; she knew the words so well. Every photograph and every single reference to her father had been removed. It was as if he had been wiped out of her life for a second time. Worse. It was as if he had never existed.

Lydia ran to the other side of her bed and picked up Joe's book. She searched frantically through it. There was nothing, nothing of their father's, nothing to remind them of him. She sat on the bed and howled with anguish. She may have hated him for what he had done to her mother, but she loved him still. She tried desperately to see his face, but it remained stubbornly vague. Soon, she wouldn't even be able to remember what he looked like, and this time there would be no photograph to reset her memory.

Chapter 15

The land documents. Lydia couldn't remember having seen them. She lay counting the minutes, counting the hours, willing the dawn to come early so that she could check whether or not they were still there in the box. Sleep had already deserted her again, driven away by the trauma of the day, when this new fear arose; the fear that Grandma Motsie had taken the documents which proved that Lydia, Joe and Kesi now owned their parents' homestead and land.

I am leaving you the documents that prove your legal entitlement to this rondavel and land upon my death. Take care of them, Lydia. Without them, you may have to fight to prove your ownership. There are those who will seize any opportunity they can to dispossess you. You are children, and vulnerable. Poverty can distort a person's judgement of what is right and what is wrong. So can wealth. Beware of trickster words and trickster smiles. They may be setting a trap and you may not see it until it is too late.

Did you know, Mama? Lydia wondered. *Were you trying to warn me about Grandma? You knew she didn't like us, but I'm sure you must have thought she would take pity on us. I'm sure you must have thought she would be kind to us when you were gone. Or did you? I don't think you could have guessed that she would be as cruel as she has been, because I think you would have found some way to protect us.*

Joe and Kesi stirred, both together. Lydia lay still, hoping for some indication that they were awake enough for her to disturb them, but it went quiet again. She was reminded of the nights when she lay awake listening to her mother's breathing, her heart skipping a beat every time her mother skipped a breath. This night was such a lonely, frightening place that she found herself willing Joe to wake up and share the burden with her. But she didn't want him to know what was worrying her, because she might be worrying about nothing. And Joe had been so deeply upset and angry when she told him about the missing photographs and words. He had wanted there and then to confront Grandma Motsie, to ask her why she hated them so much. Lydia had had to restrain him. How would he react if it were true that she had stolen their home?

She decided to wait until her brother and sister were on their way to school before she went to her mother's box. That would give her time to decide what to do if she found the papers were missing. She practically shoved them out of the door when at last they were ready. Even so, Joe hesitated by the hedge and asked once again if she was sure she would be all right on her own.

'Just go,' she said. 'I'll be fine. I'm going to see if I can borrow a spade so I can get to work on the garden.'

'I could stay and help.'

'No, Joe. You've got football training, and at least they'll give you something to eat at school.'

'What will you eat?'

'I'll see if they've got any leftovers at the store.'

'What if Grandma comes again?'

'She can't do worse than she did yesterday and I'll be ready for her this time.'

'But I should be here to protect you.'

'You'll need protection *from* me if you don't get

going,' Lydia said. She waved her fist at him, trying to disguise her frustration with mock threats.

'Shall I stay?' Kesi piped up.

'No!' Joe and Lydia cried together.

Lydia breathed a sigh of relief as her brother and sister set off down the road, but then her heart started to pound at the thought of what she might be about to discover. She pulled the box out from under the bed and sat looking at it for a moment. Then with a rush she picked it up and tipped the contents on to the bed. She distracted herself briefly by holding her mother's favourite bangle, turning it slowly in her hands, slipping it on and off her wrist. At least that was still there. She glanced at the pile of papers. There were the drawings she had done at school when she was younger, old letters from family members and some photographs that were still intact. She sifted through them one by one, slowly at first, then more and more frantically.

The land documents weren't there. Lydia grabbed Joe's school papers and looked through those as well, though she knew she wouldn't find them. She knew the answer already. The documents had gone. Grandma Motsie had stolen them. She realised then that her mother's watch had gone too. Her mother's treasured watch, bought for her by her husband when he had been earning good money and wanted to spoil her.

Lydia was too numb even to weep. She sat on the bed and stared at the walls. What was the point of trying any more? Their grandmother seemed determined to destroy them and they had no weapons with which to fight against her. How long would it be before she arrived, waving the documents in their faces, demanding that they leave their home for ever? And if Lydia went to her grandmother's house to beg her to give the papers back? She couldn't do it. In any case, she knew what Grandma Motsie's reaction would be at any suggestion that she had stolen them. The only other possibility was for her to inform her grandmother that the papers had gone and beg her to help find them.

Lydia stood up. What was she thinking of? She had swallowed her pride too many times before. She had behaved in the way expected of someone of her age and tried to be respectful. Never, never would she go begging to Grandma Motsie again. She would rather beg on the streets of the nearest town. If only there were someone in the village she could talk to, but who would believe that their grandmother had stolen from her own family, and what revenge would the old woman take if they attempted to expose her? Lydia returned everything to her mother's box and set about the chores. She needed to keep herself occupied, to stop herself from thinking about what was going to happen.

That day, Lydia cleaned the rondavel like it had never been cleaned before. She stripped the sheets from the bed, ready to take them to the river to be washed. She plumped up the shabby pillows and left them to air on the chair outside. She wiped the stove until all the cooking spills had gone, then scrubbed the wall behind it to remove the stains. She took the rug outside and beat it with a small branch – at least, as much as she dared, because it was becoming threadbare. She rubbed so hard at the tin-topped table that she could see her face in it. She collected twigs and leaves, tied them together decoratively and hung them from a nail on the inside of the door. She pinned a picture Kesi had drawn on to the wall, and another that she had painted herself before she stopped going to school. Under the bed, she found a carving that Joe had spent hours whittling away at. She gave it pride of place on the polished table. She swept every centimetre of the floor, and then swept it again. As soon as she had finished, she went outside and swept the yard with the same thinning brush, until her back and knees protested when she straightened them up. It was an act of sheer defiance, a statement saying: 'This is ours. You have no right to it.'

Lydia stood for a moment in the doorway, exhausted but satisfied. The one thing she couldn't bring herself to tackle was the garden. She couldn't bear the thought that any work she did might be wasted; that any vegetables she grew might be served up on Grandma Motsie's table. She knew she had to face the problem of how they were going to feed themselves, but for the moment she pushed it aside. She pushed aside too her fear that her grandmother might turn up while she was away washing the sheets. She had to chance it. She couldn't become a prisoner in her own home.

It was a much chillier day, Lydia noticed, once she was away from the rondavel. A blustery wind from the hills reminded her that the seasons were changing. She shivered and, when she tried to wrap her cardigan further round herself, discovered again how much she had grown. She mused on the fact that her body was still able to extend itself, even though she was eating so little. If it kept on, she would be all height and no width, like the tall reeds that marshalled the edge of the river.

She was pleased to find once again that nobody else

was about when she reached the river. She stepped on to a rock, bent down and swished the sheets backwards and forward in the water until they were soaking wet. She took her last small piece of soap from her pocket and worked it into them, then dropped them back into the water to rinse. She stood up and began to pull them ashore, wringing them out at the same time, when she sensed a movement behind her.

Lydia looked round to see Jabu squatting underneath a tree on the edge of the path, smoking a cigarette. She flinched and turned away from him, gathering up the sheets as fast as she could. One of them caught on a bramble. Lydia shook it to loosen it, but it held fast. She could feel the panic welling up inside her. In her desperation to flee, she tugged too hard and the sheet tore for a second time before dragging along the dusty ground.

'Can I help?' she heard Jabu say.

She ignored him.

'I promise I'll keep my distance,' he continued, 'and I'm sorry I upset you the other day.'

Lydia carried on ignoring him as she rolled the sheets into a bundle. All she could think about was how to get past him and away up the path. She was terrified that if she went anywhere near him he might grab at her.

141

How quickly could he jump to his feet if she made a dash for it? Could she run fast enough? She doubted it. The path was too narrow for her to keep out of his reach, and the scrub was too dense on either side for her to be able to push her way through. Her only option was the river. She was a good swimmer, but she wouldn't be able to swim with the sheets, and she couldn't leave them behind because they were the only ones they had.

'That was a good shot you took at me with the pot. Only just missed my head.'

Is he expecting me to apologise? Lydia wondered.

'I told the old lady it was an accident,' he continued. 'Couldn't have her beating you up about it.'

And now, is he expecting me to express my gratitude?

'I think you'll need to wash those sheets again, won't you?'

Lydia felt that he was mocking her. 'Please, let me go past,' she said weakly, without looking at him.

'Am I stopping you? I'm not stopping you. Off you go. I just wanted you to know that I don't mean you any harm.'

Lydia took a hesitant step in his direction. He stood up as she did so. She stopped. He leant against the tree, took a long suck at his cigarette, blew the smoke theatrically into the air, threw the butt on to the ground and stamped on it.

'Don't want to cause a fire, do I?' he grinned. 'Don't look so serious, Lydia. I said I meant you no harm.'

'You're playing games with me,' Lydia muttered.

'No games. I'm just offering you my help.'

'I don't need your help.'

'I think you do. And if you don't now, you soon will. You see, your grandmother tells me things.'

'What sort of things?' Lydia asked, in spite of herself.

'Oh, things like, she's worn out from caring for her grandchildren and can't cope with it at her time of life. Things like, she can no longer afford to keep you, which is why she was helping you train for a good job. Things like, she spent so much money on medicines for your mother, that she needs to make sure she keeps some for herself, given her poor health.'

'She's lying. She didn't spend a cent on medicines for my mother. My mother went without so that there would be money for us when she died.' Lydia was outraged that her grandmother should make such claims in order to justify her meanness.

'Things like, she wouldn't have to pay her staff so much if she could offer them somewhere to live.

143

Things like, if her grandchildren's homestead were available her staff could live there. Otherwise, the homestead might have to be sold to pay the family's debts.'

Jabu stared at her, waiting for her reaction. Lydia bit her lip hard to stop it from trembling. She was trying to decipher what he was telling her. The words seemed to dance around, refusing to fit together. And then she had just one thought: to get away from there. To get away from Jabu and the games he was playing with her mind. She held the wet sheets tightly against her chest and strode up the path, head down. When she could see his feet out of the corner of her eye, she broke into a run. She ran as fast as she could, on and on until she reached the rondavel, where she lurched inside and closed the door behind her. She dropped the sheets to the floor and sat on a chair, struggling to catch her breath, petrified that Jabu might be coming after her.

What did it all mean? What was her grandmother up to? Was it her plan to let Jabu live in their rondavel and, if so, what was to happen to them? Was it all Jabu's doing? Was he manipulating the old woman for his own benefit, or were they plotting together? Did Jabu know about the stolen documents? Had he helped to steal them? How could Grandma Motsie betray her own family in the way that Jabu suggested she might?

It was a while before Lydia was able to stand up, a while before the disquiet in her stomach had eased sufficiently for her not to feel that she would be sick if she moved. She had completely lost track of what time of day it was and hoped that Joe and Kesi wouldn't be back too soon. She peered cautiously through the window to check that Jabu wasn't lurking outside, then picked up the sheets. They were covered in dirt. They would have to stay that way. She opened the door, ready to hang them out to dry. At that very moment, it started to rain.

Chapter 16

Lydia didn't dare to leave the homestead during the next few days. She kept from Joe her discovery that the land documents had been stolen, and decided that he must never know about what Jabu had told her. As the weeks passed by, her brother was becoming more and more protective of her. She was scared of what he might do if he learned the full extent of their grand-mother's treachery.

Joe — what can I tell you about Joe, Lydia? He is a boy, and sometimes boys need to be protected from themselves. He is so young now, but he will grow up quickly when I am gone. He will want to step into his father's shoes. Allow him to do that slowly, but keep hold of the reins so that you can haul him back when he tries to go too far in one direction or the other. Boys can be hot-headed and wild, especially when they lose their role model. Or they can become sombre and serious, missing out on the freedoms of childhood. Try to steer your brother down a middle path. Make sure he has time to have fun, but allow him to feel that he has an important part to play in the survival of our family.

What a burden I am placing on you. In your darkest hours, Lydia, keep climbing that tree.

Every minute of every day, Lydia expected Jabu to turn up. She jumped at the slightest unusual sound, running inside and shutting the door behind her if she heard a truck on the road above or footsteps on the path to the river. She only felt safe when her brother and sister were at home, because she didn't think Jabu would bother her then. As for Grandma Motsie, Lydia could only wait to see what she would do. The worst thing was that she had no choice but to work on the garden, even if they were never to benefit from it. Joe was determined that they would grow their own food again. He even came back from school with a spade he had borrowed from Mrs Sibiya and a torn packet of cabbage seeds, with half of them missing, that he had scrounged from the store.

'Come on, Liddy,' he urged her, when he felt she wasn't pulling her weight. 'At least we've got something better than a bent fork to dig with now, and the ground's getting soft. At least we've got something to grow.'

'I don't like cabbage,' pouted Kesi.

'All the more for us then,' Joe answered back. 'Anyway, Mr Namile said if I did a bit of work for him he'd give me lots more seeds.'

'When will you have time to do work for him, Joe? You've got school and homework and football, and we need you here.' Lydia was aware that she was sounding negative. She was cross with herself when she saw Joe's face tighten.

'Why do you keep putting problems in the way?' he said. 'It's like you don't want us to sort the garden out.'

'I'm sorry,' Lydia said quickly. 'I just keep worrying about your schoolwork.'

'I'm more worried about starving. Have you seen how skinny you are, Liddy?'

'It's only because I'm growing,' Lydia said defensively.

'It's not only that. It's because you don't eat all day and then all you have in the evening is the scraps we bring back from school.'

'I'm all right,' Lydia said firmly, 'and I don't want you to worry. It's up to me to sort things out. You're too young to work. You should be out playing like other children.'

'But I'm not like other children, am I? Except the ones who are orphans as well. And some of them have to go to work too, unless they've got family.'

Lydia couldn't argue any longer. She knew she was losing the battle. Joe wanted to feel that he could make a difference to them. All she could do was to make sure that he kept going with his football and met up with his friends sometimes. She admired the dogged way in which he had set his mind to making the garden his priority. He was still only nine, yet in some respects he had more resolve than she had. At least she could protect him from the knowledge of his grandmother's treachery. And she could do her best to support his efforts regardless of her fears that they might be wasted.

And so, each day, when she had finished the household chores, Lydia went out into the garden and dug and weeded, until her hands were covered in blisters. If only it would stop raining. Every clump of weeds that she pulled from the ground came with its roots holding fast to a sodden clod of earth. Every patch of ground that she managed to clear turned quickly into a mess of mud that clung to her feet. She sowed some of the cabbage seeds and found them, soon afterwards, floating in a pool of water. She sowed them again, and a third time, until at last they stayed put.

Their efforts were rewarded when, a few days later, Joe came in from the garden, whooping with glee, to tell her that the cabbages were growing.

'We did it, Liddy, we did it!' he cried.

'I want to see,' squealed Kesi, running outside.

Lydia followed her and bent down to look. Sure enough, smatterings of pin-sized green shoots were poking up through the wet soil. She ran the swollen palm of her hand gently over the tops of them. It was worth all the pain to see this tiny beginning of new life.

'I'll go now and help Mr Namile mend his fence, so that we can have some more seeds to sow,' said Joe.

'Thanks, Joe,' said Lydia. 'Thanks for helping.'

'And me,' said Kesi. 'I helped too.'

'You did most of it, Liddy,' said Joe.

'You've kept me going,' replied Lydia.

As if to show that things were getting better, the rain stopped and the skies cleared. It was much colder though. They would need to start collecting firewood for the winter months. While Joe was out and Kesi had gone to play with a friend, Lydia ventured away from the homestead for the first time since her encounter with Jabu. She needed to take some washing down to the river, but she didn't dare go that far. Instead she walked a short distance along another path to an area of brushwood, where she could pick up some kindling.

It felt good to leave the homestead, even if she hadn't gone very far and she knew that at some point she would have to go much further afield to fetch wood. It was a relief too to look up at a clear sky. Even the moon was visible, just a sliver, like a fragment of lace. Lydia scarcely dared to believe that their luck might be changing, but a tiny seed of hope settled deep inside her. Somewhere close by a bird was singing, a sound she hadn't heard for what seemed like months, or was it just that she hadn't been listening? She listened now, peering through the bushes at the same time to see where it was perched. It was singing its heart out,

151

and she waited for another bird to answer, to no avail. At last, she spotted a flash of colour which confirmed what she had thought, that the singer was a crested barbet. It flew off almost as soon as she saw it. She hoped that she hadn't frightened it away from its nest.

As soon as she had filled the basket, Lydia hurried back home, a sharp breeze nipping at her bare arms and legs. She closed the door behind her, prepared the kindling for the fire and began to sweep the floor. She was hungry. She was always hungry, but it was worse at weekends when Joe and Kesi couldn't bring her scraps from school. She would have to see if she could find a job, but most of the villagers were so poor themselves that she doubted anyone would be able to offer her anything. Joe was lucky that Mr Namile had asked him to help with the fence, and she was grateful for that. She hoped that with the money he earned they might be able to buy some food to last them for a few days.

There was a knock on the door. Lydia froze. Another knock, louder this time. Lydia pressed herself against the wall by the door, so that if anyone came to the window, she wouldn't be seen unless they leaned right in. Her eyes fixed on the handle, half expecting it to start turning. And then she heard a voice. A girl's voice.

'Lydia, are you there?'

'Mandisa?' Lydia breathed. She pulled open the door. Her friend stood awkwardly before her.

'My mother, she . . .'

'I know,' said Lydia. 'I came by and there were lots of villagers, so I know.'

Mandisa burst into tears. Lydia put her arm round her, led her indoors and sat down with her on the bed.

'It's hard enough,' Mandisa said between sobs, 'but people are saying things. Horrible things.'

'Those people are not kind,' said Lydia. 'You mustn't listen to those people. They are not your friends.'

'I don't know why Mama died, so why do they think they know?'

'They don't know,' said Lydia. 'It's private, so how can they? People can be very cruel, especially when they're scared for themselves. Especially when they don't understand.'

For a while, neither of them spoke, both of them thinking their own thoughts, until Mandisa said, 'It hurts so much, Lydia. I didn't know it would hurt so much.'

Lydia pulled her friend closer and held her hand tight.

'I'm so frightened that she's going to disappear completely, that I won't be able to remember anything about her.'

'Did she leave anything for you?' Lydia asked carefully.

Mandisa gazed at her quizzically with her bloodshot eyes. 'We've got her clothes and her jewellery,' she said.

'Try holding them up sometimes and imagining her in them.'

'Is that what you do? Does it really help?'

Lydia shifted uncomfortably. 'Mama left me a book as well, a memory book, with things she wanted me to know about and things she wanted me to remember. I read it and it makes me feel better.'

Mandisa nodded her head slowly. 'Did she know she was going to die, then?'

It was Lydia's turn to nod. 'Yes,' she said. 'She knew. We all knew. It was like with my father.'

'I don't think my mother knew,' whispered Mandisa. 'But I did. Simba told me, but I knew anyway.'

'Will you go back to school?' Lydia asked.

Mandisa shrugged her shoulders. 'I don't know,' she said. 'I don't want to at the moment. I can't face everyone. My grandma's trying to make me. She says it'll help to take my mind off things. Things. What she means is Mama, but why should I want to take my mind off her? Simba won't talk about it – won't talk about Mama. It's like they're trying to forget her and want me to as well.'

'Perhaps it's too painful for them.'

'And it's not for me?'

'You know I don't mean that,' Lydia sighed inadvertently.

'I'm annoying you.' Mandisa jumped to her feet and made for the door.

'You're not annoying me,' said Lydia, quickly jumping to her feet as well. 'I'm pleased you're here. I need to talk to somebody. I need to talk to you.'

'Hmm, I don't see what use I can be.'

Mandisa was so full of self-pity, understandably, that Lydia almost changed her mind about sharing confidences with her. But she had kept everything bottled up for so long that it threatened to shoot out in spite of herself. 'Please stay,' she said.

Mandisa nodded and they sat down again. There was silence between them, as Lydia tried to find the right words to tell Mandisa what was happening to her, without discrediting her grandmother. Grandma Motsie was still family, but then she blurted it all out, words and fears and emotions tumbling over each other in their efforts to express themselves. By the time she had finished, Lydia was exhausted.

Mandisa was shocked. 'You mean, you might have to leave here? You might not have anywhere to live?'

'I think Grandma means to let Jabu live here.'

'But he's not even family.'

'I think she expects us to live with him or move out.' Lydia could hardly bring herself to voice her greatest concerns.

'That's awful!' gasped Mandisa. 'Why would she do that?'

'Because she's old and doesn't want the bother of us.' Lydia didn't say it in an accusing way. She even tried to make it sound as if it was excusable as her worries about her family's honour pressed upon her again.

'She can't just move someone else into your home.'

'No, she can't, because I won't let her. I'd rather go and beg than give in to her plans. But I've got to think about Joe and Kesi as well.'

'Who is this Jabu? Has he put your grandmother up

to all of this? My grandma would never dream of behaving in such a way.'

'I don't know,' Lydia sighed, 'but I'm terrified of bumping into him again. I don't trust him.'

'I wish I could help,' said Mandisa.

'You have helped, just by sharing it with me. There's nothing else anyone can do. I've just got to wait and see what happens.'

'Well, it's not fair and I'm going to ask Grandma if there's anything she can do.'

'Please don't, Mandisa,' Lydia said. 'It will only cause more trouble.'

They sat a little while longer, talking about school and friends. Then they talked about their mothers and all the good times they had spent with them. Lydia was surprised at how much calmer she felt now that someone else knew what she was going through. She realised once again how valuable Mandisa's friendship was to her, and resolved to visit her as often as she could to help her cope with her grief.

When Mandisa stood and said she needed to collect some wood for her grandmother, Lydia was reluctant to let her go.

'Come and see me again, whenever you like,' she said, 'and I'll come and see you too.'

'I feel a bit better, thanks,' said Mandisa. 'I can see Mama smiling.'

'She'll always be there, smiling down at you. You just have to gather together the wispy threads of your memories and you'll find her.'

'Is that what your mama said?'

'No. It's what I say,' grinned Lydia.

Joe returned late that afternoon and strutted around like a prize cockerel. 'Four packets of seeds, Liddy. Look, I've got carrots, beans and maize. And I've got some potato tubers and enough food for today and tomorrow.'

'That's great, Joe. You're a star.' Lydia gave him a big hug. 'I'd better get cooking.'

'Can I help?' asked Kesi excitedly.

'Course you can.'

'Don't use too much, will you, Liddy?' said Joe. 'We want to make it last.'

'Listen to you, Mr Practical,' laughed Lydia. 'I'll stretch it as far as I can, but we deserve a bit of a celebration. It's been a good day.'

'I had a good day,' grinned Kesi. 'Thembelephi says I'm her best friend ever.'

'And is she your best friend ever?' asked Lydia.

'Ever and ever and ever!' Kesi leapt on to the bed and did a somersault. 'When can she come here?'

'Whenever you like,' said Lydia.

'Just make sure I'm out,' frowned Joe. 'One five-year-old is enough for anybody.'

'I'm nearly six,' protested Kesi.

'And even more of a pain than ever,' Joe rejoined. He began to tickle her. She shrieked for mercy, but when he didn't stop she sank her teeth into his shoulder.

'Ow!' he cried. 'What did you do that for? She bit me, Liddy.'

'I think that serves you right for not stopping when she told you,' laughed Lydia.

'I can see the teethmarks,' Joe pouted.

'You'll live,' said Lydia. 'Now, come on you two. No more messing around while I'm cooking.'

They set the table and played cards while a saucepan of stew bubbled on the stove. The delicious smells were almost too much to bear. Kesi kept asking when it would be ready, and Lydia was tempted to serve it up early to quell the eager lurching of her stomach. She held firm though, which made the meal taste even better when she declared, finally, that they could eat.

159

They piled their plates high, but there was still plenty left afterwards. Lydia saw the look of pride on Joe's face and was happy for him.

That night, before she went to sleep, she spoke softly to her mother. 'Things are going to be all right, Mama. I don't know how, and I don't know when, but today was a start.'

Chapter 17

A box of vegetables and rice appeared on their doorstep in the middle of the night. Joe nearly tripped over it the next morning when he went out to fetch the water. He rushed back indoors to tell Lydia. They stood over it, all three of them, wondering where on earth it had come from. They searched for a note, but there was nothing to tell them who had put it there.

'I don't think we should touch them,' said Lydia.

'Why not?' Joe protested. 'There's nothing wrong with them.'

'We don't know who put them there.'

'Someone kind put them there,' said Joe.

'Why don't they say who they are then?' asked Lydia.

Joe shrugged his shoulders. 'I don't know, but what

are we going to do, throw them away? Just because we had lots to eat yesterday and there's some left for today, it doesn't mean we won't be starving again by the end of the week.'

Lydia acknowledged that Joe was right, but she was uneasy about accepting a gift when they had no idea who it was from. 'Perhaps we can just leave them outside till we need them,' she said.

'What, so somebody can steal them?' Joe exclaimed. 'It's no good pretending we might not need them, because you know we will.'

'We would have managed if this hadn't happened,' Lydia replied weakly.

'No, we wouldn't,' argued Joe. 'We hardly had anything to eat before and it was getting worse every day. You're getting really skinny, Liddy, you know you are, and it's not just because you're growing. I might only be your little brother, but I can see that there's hardly anything left of my big sister.'

Lydia caved in and allowed the box to be taken inside. She decided she should be grateful, and hoped they would quickly discover who had left it for them so that they could thank them. At least it meant that for a few days they didn't need to worry about what they were going to eat, and could focus on finishing the garden ready for the new seeds.

During all this time, none of them had seen any sign of Grandma Motsie. Lydia tried not to think about her, but whenever she picked up her mother's book and saw the torn pages, she couldn't help but be reminded of her. She was certain her grandmother would appear sooner or later and she was dreading that moment, but she refused to be cowed by thoughts of it.

Lydia went to visit Mandisa, keeping a lookout all the way in case Jabu was lurking somewhere. She was pleased to find that her friend was more cheerful. Mandisa's grandmother, Grandma Shandu, was with her. Lydia watched them together. They were almost like mother and daughter, so obviously deeply fond of each other. Grandma Shandu was kind to Lydia as well. Lydia guessed that Mandisa had told her something of her situation, but she didn't know how much.

'Never feel you are alone, Lydia, child,' she said. 'You have friends here, and I would not be able to sleep in my bed at night if I thought you were going hungry, or worse.'

'Thank you, Mrs Shandu,' Lydia said, 'but I'm sure you have enough to cope with with your own grand-children.'

'Ha! Simba, he's not a child any more. He's like a grown man, though I know that he is hurting inside. Of course, Mandisa, she's a lot of work, such hard work, especially at my time of life.' She grinned a toothy grin at Lydia.

'I'm not hard work,' Mandisa protested hotly.

'You see, she has such a temper on her,' Mrs Shandu continued. 'Anyway, let's be serious. Has anybody told you that you can get a government grant to help you with food?'

Lydia nodded her head. 'Mrs Dlamini told me, but what with everything else —'

'It's not very much, and it never arrives on time, but it's better than nothing.'

'Lydia says someone left a box of food outside her door,' Mandisa chipped in.

'Well, then, she must have a guardian angel looking after her, but it won't do any harm to have the government do its bit as well. You're three young children on your own and you're entitled to govern-ment support. You may have to prove that nobody in your family is helping you, though. And if somebody is claiming a grant to support you, then you may have a bit of a problem.'

Mrs Shandu stared searchingly at Lydia. Lydia wanted to open up to her, but she couldn't bring herself to be so disloyal to her grandmother, even though she immediately began to wonder if Grandma Motsie was indeed receiving a government grant to support her grandchildren. She put it out of her mind. She knew she wasn't going to apply for a grant. What would be the point? They would never be able to prove that they had no support from their grandmother. She expressed her gratitude, nevertheless, and went home feeling cheered that she had someone to talk to.

Another week passed by, during which they finished the last of the food that had been left for them. Lydia was beginning to panic about where their next meal was going to come from, when another box appeared outside the door. This time, there was a note attached to it. She unfolded it and read: *I hope you enjoyed my first gift. I thought you might need some more help, though I see that the garden is looking promising. Congratulations. Your good friend, Jabu.*

Lydia dropped it as if it had burned her fingers. She ran outside to be sick. Joe followed her out, clutching the note, Kesi behind him, looking scared.

'Throw them away, Joe, please,' Lydia begged. She was shaking all over.

Joe didn't argue. He grabbed the box and hurried down the path with it. Kesi took Lydia's hand.

'Are those vegetables not nice?' she asked.

Lydia shook her head. She slumped down against the wall of the rondavel and closed her eyes.

'Don't die, Liddy,' Kesi whispered.

Lydia couldn't answer. She heard Joe come back and Kesi asking him what was wrong with her. Then she felt him slide down next to her.

'I got rid of them,' he said. 'What are we going to do?'

'We'll manage,' she murmured.

'About Jabu, I mean.'

'Perhaps we should just go away from here.'

'Where would we go?'

'Anywhere.'

Joe fell silent. After a while, he said, 'I don't want to go away, Liddy. This is our home. I've got friends here, and what about school?'

Lydia stirred herself. 'School,' she said. 'You're going to be late.'

'I think we should stay with you today,' he said.

'I want to stay with you, Liddy,' Kesi added.

'No,' said Lydia firmly. 'We should carry on as if nothing has happened.'

Joe could tell by the set of Lydia's lips that her mind was made up. He didn't want to antagonise her, but when he was ready to leave and while Kesi was out of earshot, he said, 'We should do something about that Jabu. We should report him or something.'

'And say what?' asked Lydia. 'That he has been giving us boxes of food?'

'That he said things about Mama and we don't trust him.'

'It's not a crime. And who'd listen?'

'He keeps bothering us. He shouldn't be allowed to bother us.'

'You should go to school, Joe, now, and leave me to deal with it.'

What am I going to do, though? she asked herself over and over again as soon as they had gone.

The arrival of the second box of food on their doorstep had killed the seed of optimism which she had been nurturing. It had grown, along with the seedlings in their garden and the revival of her friendship with Mandisa. She half expected those to die too, even though when she looked across the garden she could see that the seedlings were flourishing. They brought her no joy. She knew the time must be approaching when Grandma Motsie would pounce. She felt so utterly exhausted at the thought of it.

'What would you want me to do, Mama?' she whispered.

Fight, she heard. It wasn't her mother's voice, it was her own. *Fight*, it said, *until you haven't an ounce of strength left in your body. Fight, because if you don't you will never be able to live with yourself. You will never be able to say that you did everything you possibly could. Never mind that you're fighting against impossible odds. Never mind that you may wind up worse off than when you started. At least you will know that you tried, that you didn't give up, that you didn't give in. What are you waiting for, Lydia?*

Chapter 18

It had started to rain again when Lydia left the home-stead, but that didn't deter her. She ran up the path to the road, then marched along the edge, ignoring the spray from passing trucks and the whoops and whistles from workers sitting in the back of them. She fixed her eyes on a spot on the horizon and headed determinedly towards it. She blanked everything from her mind. If someone spoke to her, she wouldn't have known. If an animal crossed in front of her, she wouldn't have seen it. That morning, nobody could have deflected her from what she had resolved to do.

You'll have to be strong, Lydia.

When, at last, Grandma Motsie's house came into view, Lydia stopped for a moment to catch her breath.

She leant against a tree, wiped the rain from her face and smoothed down her clothes. Even from where she stood, she could see Jabu working on her grandmother's land. Her heart missed a beat, but he had lost the power to frighten her. In her present mood, nothing could frighten her. She set off again, walking steadily in the direction of the house. She glanced sideways once and knew that Jabu had spotted her. She saw him down his tools, wipe his hands on his trousers and head towards her.

'Hey, Lydia!' he called.

She didn't reply, just carried on walking.

'Have you forgiven me yet?'

She left his question hanging in the air.

'You're looking well,' he said. He was quite close to her now. 'It must be the food I left for you.'

'We threw it away,' Lydia informed him. She allowed herself to watch for a reaction, and was pleased to see that he was taken aback.

'Now, why would you do that?' he asked.

'Because we'd rather eat poison, what do you think?' said Lydia.

'And there's me just trying to be friendly,' he said.

Lydia stepped up to her grandmother's door and knocked loudly. Jabu strolled back to his work, whistling tunelessly. The door opened. Lydia registered the look of shock on the old woman's face. It fuelled her strength to know that she had stolen the initiative from her.

'I've come to ask for our land documents back,' she said firmly.

'What do you mean?' Grandma Motsie was flustered. She hadn't expected this.

'You took them from us, didn't you, and all the pictures of Baba? I'd like them back, please.'

'Do you know what you're saying?'

'Yes. I do.'

'And do you think it's right for a young girl to talk to her elders like this?' Grandma Motsie was attempting to regain the upper hand.

'I'm being perfectly polite,' said Lydia.

'And your accusations are monstrous!' the old woman finally exploded.

'So is taking things from your grandchildren,' Lydia said, trying to stay calm.

'They have been returned to their rightful owner. That homestead was bought by my son.'

'He was our father, and my mother paid for it too.' Lydia could feel the anger she was holding inside beginning to boil over. 'Why are you doing this?

Why do you want to leave your own grandchildren with nowhere to live?'

'I am not so very cruel,' Grandma Motsie snapped. 'Who said that I was going to make you leave?'

It was Lydia's turn to look momentarily surprised.

'I would not deprive my grandchildren of a roof over their heads,' her grandmother continued. 'I am simply making it available to someone else as well.'

'You mean Jabu, don't you?'

'He's a good man. He looks after me well. He would look after you well, and he needs somewhere to live.'

'Then let him live here.'

'That would hardly be proper, Lydia.'

'And you think it would be proper for him to live with us?'

'As a lodger, yes, perfectly proper, and a perfect way out of the predicament you find yourself in.'

'When Jabu told me that's what you had planned, I never believed you would be capable of it,' Lydia said quietly. 'Now I know.'

'I have your interests at heart. It's your own stubbornness and those puffed-up ideas your mother has filled you with that prevent you from seeing it.'

Lydia couldn't listen any more. 'When will we have to leave?' she asked.

Grandma Motsie stared straight into her eyes. 'I don't think it will come to that,' she said.

'When?' Lydia almost shouted it this time.

'Winter's coming,' her grandmother replied.

'We'll fight you, Grandma. We'll fight you every step of the way.'

The old woman turned her back on her and closed the door.

Lydia hesitated, then turned herself to leave. Jabu was standing at the end of the garden, leaning on a hoe, a cigarette clutched between the fingers of one hand. He bowed his head to her – mockingly, she thought. She hurried along the path. She had accomplished what she came for. All she wanted now was to be as far away from there as possible.

She didn't go straight home. She set off for Mandisa's homestead. She wanted the comfort of being with a friend. The rain was lashing down as she walked back through the village and up the hill on the other side. It was cold too. Winter was closing in fast, the first snows already highlighting the tops of the mountains against the dull grey sky. Lydia wished she had worn her cardigan, but she hadn't noticed the cold when she left for Grandma Motsie's that morning. She hurried on, and at last saw Mandisa's homestead opening out in front of her.

When she knocked on the door, it was Mrs Shandu who opened it. She greeted Lydia with a big smile and welcomed her in.

'Mandisa's gone to school,' she said happily, as she handed Lydia a cloth to dry herself. 'She made the decision herself.'

Lydia hid her disappointment that her friend wasn't there. 'I'm glad for her,' she said.

'You should return to school too, Lydia,' Mrs Shandu said. 'Is there anything I can do to help you?'

Lydia shook her head, swallowing hard.

'Here, child, take this with you.' Mrs Shandu handed her a bowl of nsima. 'Get some food inside you and things will seem better. And borrow this coat of mine before you freeze to death.'

'Thank you, Mrs Shandu. You're so kind,' said Lydia.

She turned to leave, but Mrs Shandu stopped her, saying, 'Lydia, if ever you find yourself without a roof over your head, you are welcome here, and Joe and Kesi. I can't offer you much, but I won't see a young family homeless.'

Lydia managed to choke out her gratitude before setting off along the path again, tears rolling down her cheeks.

She was exhausted by the time she arrived home, not

just physically but emotionally. She lay down on the bed and played back through her mind everything that had happened. She should have felt elated because she had stood up to Grandma Motsie and made her aware that she would fight her. The trouble was that it had all been words. She had no idea how to fight her, except that she was sure there must be a way to prove that the homestead belonged to her. Her heart warmed when she thought about Mrs Shandu and the kind offer she had made. It had been a good day, she had to believe that, but she didn't know what she should do next.

She leant over the edge of the bed and picked up her mother's book. She hadn't looked at it very often since Grandma Motsie had defaced it. Perhaps she hadn't felt the need to either – so much of what her mother had written was embedded deep within her. She turned the pages slowly, carefully, familiar phrases and sentences catching her eye every so often, until she came to the very last page her mother had written. She hadn't read it as often as the other pages. She had found its finality too painful.

These will be my last words, Lydia. I am looking at you as I write, at your gentle face, your sensitive hands. My love for you is overwhelming. You have made me proud, and I leave knowing that you will find a way to flourish. I want you to remember that even when I am no longer with you, my spirit will be guiding you every minute of every day. You will never be alone. When you have finished crying for me, search deep inside yourself and you will find me. We will always be together, Lydia, even when my life is over. I love you, Lydia.

Chapter 19

Lydia was woken in the night by her sister's coughing. She lay still, waiting to see if she would cough again. On the other side of the bed, Joe was snoring loudly. Lydia moved closer to her sister, trying to hear the sound of her breathing. Kesi's mouth was open and small rasping noises were coming from it. Lydia touched her forehead. It was warm, but not hot. She decided that there was nothing to worry about. A cold, perhaps, but nothing more.

By early morning, Kesi was coughing regularly and had become restless in her sleep. When she woke, she complained of a headache. Lydia made her drink lots of water and told her she was to stay in bed.

'Aren't I going to school?' she asked.

'No,' said Lydia. 'Not if you're not well.'

'Will you stay here with me?'

'I'm not going anywhere. Now, you just rest and then you'll get better quicker.'

Kesi closed her eyes and turned over on to her side, but she soon rolled back again. 'Mama got a cough, didn't she?'

'Yes, she did, but it was a different sort of cough,' said Lydia.

'Did she get hot?'

'Sometimes.'

'I'm hot,' said Kesi.

'Let's take that blanket off you then.' Lydia pulled back the blanket, then felt Kesi's forehead. It was warmer but not burning. 'You need to try and sleep, Kes.'

'What if I don't wake up?' Kesi's voice was quavering.

'You will wake up because I shall prod you and tickle you until you do.'

'Did you do that to Mama?'

'It was different with Mama,' Lydia tried to reassure her. 'Mama was a little bit ill for quite a long time, but she didn't cough at all. And she was still able to do lots of things. Then she became more ill and started to cough. It's not the same with you. You've become ill very quickly and you're going to get better very quickly. Come on, I'll lie down with you.'

Kesi coughed then snuggled up to Lydia. Lydia was

pleased when she heard her breathing soften and felt her body relax. She lay there for a little while longer, just to be sure that her sister was asleep, then extricated herself and went outside.

It was a beautiful day, cold but sunny. The garden was full of promise. The shoots from the seeds they had planted looked strong and healthy. Lydia walked between the rows, bending down to pull up a weed or remove a slug. By the spring they would have plenty of vegetables to eat and some to sell as well. They would be able to buy more seeds, different seeds. She would be able to buy materials to weave rugs or make pots. If only they could stay there. As soon as Kesi was well, she would go to the authorities in town to plead her case. Somebody there, surely, would take pity on them. Somebody would decide that their parents' home should now belong to them, regardless of who held the documents. And she could ask for a grant for food as well. She set about all the household chores with renewed vigour at the thought of the fight they would put up to stay in their home.

Kesi woke, thirsty, in the middle of the day. She complained of a headache and wanted Lydia to sit with her. Lydia told her stories, made-up ones, happy ones that came from a time when their mother and father were alive. When Kesi fell asleep again, Lydia stayed with her. She realised that she was still exhausted and allowed herself to doze off. She didn't wake up until Joe came clattering in from school.

'Is Kes all right?' he asked. 'Her breathing's a bit funny.'

Lydia leant across their sister and listened, then touched her forehead. 'She seemed a bit better earlier, but she's very hot.'

'What are we going to do about her?'

'Just let her rest and make sure she drinks plenty of water. She'll be fine in a couple of days.' Lydia was confident that there was nothing to worry about. She didn't want Joe to worry either.

'I've got a letter for you,' he said, handing her an envelope.

'It must be about the school fees,' said Lydia. She opened it very slowly and read the letter.

'Come on, Lydia, what does it say?' asked Joe impatiently.

'It says that full consideration has been given to our case and that we may continue to attend the school. Our fees are going to be paid for us, Joe!' Lydia gave him a big hug.

'You said "us", Liddy,' said Joe. 'That means you too.'

'How can I go back, Joe? How will I have time to do schoolwork and all the housework and gardening as well?'

Joe didn't have time to answer before Kesi interrupted them with a violent bout of coughing. She sat up in bed and started whimpering.

'I don't feel well, Liddy,' she said.

'Poor Kes,' said Lydia. 'Sounds like you've got a bad cold or flu. I'll cook you a big bowl of the nsima Mrs Shandu gave us. That'll make you feel better.'

'I don't want to eat,' Kesi mumbled. 'My throat's all sore.'

She starting coughing again and spat a dollop of phlegm on to the bed.

'Yuck!' cried Joe. 'It's all green.'

Lydia was beginning to be concerned, but she didn't want her brother and sister to see. 'Don't make such a fuss,' she aimed at Joe, while she fetched a cloth to wipe the blanket. 'Can you go and fetch some more water, instead of standing there pulling faces?'

'Smells,' said Kesi, pulling faces herself.

'It's because you've got a bit of an infection,' said Lydia. 'Lie there quietly and try to rest.'

'Will I be able to go back to school?'

'Of course you will, and nobody can stop you now.'

'Grandma tried to stop us, didn't she, Liddy?'

Lydia nodded, stroking Kesi's frizz of hair.

'Will Grandma come to see me because I'm ill?'

'I don't know, Kes. She's always so busy.'

'I don't want her to come, Liddy. She'll say I'm making a fuss and I'm not.' Kesi started to cough again and complained that she couldn't breathe properly.

'Try to sleep,' said Lydia, 'and don't you worry about Grandma. I won't let her be horrible to you.'

'I can't sleep if I cough.'

'Try turning on your side and see if that helps.'

Kesi did as she was told, but her cough became more and more persistent and her breathing more shallow. When Joe came back, Lydia made her drink some of the fresh water. She drank a little, then refused to have any more because it hurt to swallow.

'Please, Kes, just a drop more,' Lydia pleaded.

Kesi lifted her head and took a sip. Most of it trickled out of the side of her mouth. She lay back down and closed her eyes. Lydia tucked the blanket round her, but it wasn't long before she kicked it off, murmuring that she was too hot.

'Will she be all right?' Joe whispered when they had moved away from the bed. 'Shouldn't we get a doctor?'

'The clinic's not open for days, you know that, and how would we get her there?' said Lydia. 'I'm sure she'll be better by the morning.'

'What if she's not?' Joe sounded really anxious. 'What if she gets worse in the night?'

'I'll stay awake,' Lydia assured him, but as Joe expressed his own fears, he was filling her with doubt. A few more minutes passed, before she said quietly, 'I know it's a long way, Joe, and it's nearly dark, but could you run to Mrs Shandu and ask her advice?'

Joe shot out of the door without a word. Lydia lit the lamps and squeezed Kesi's hand. There was no response, so more to keep herself occupied than because she was hungry, she began to prepare something to eat. As she waited for the water to boil, she couldn't help feeling that they were destined never to find happiness. Even the smallest happinesses were snatched away the minute they were given, like the news about the school fees. The seeds in the garden should have brought happiness, but however heartening it was to see them growing, they had no future as a family while Grandma Motsie was hatching her plans. The optimism she had felt just a few hours earlier had buried itself under this new crisis.

'Tell me another story, Liddy.'

Kesi was struggling to sit up in bed. Lydia took her another drink, which she sipped slowly.

'How are you feeling, Kes?' she asked.

'Bit better. Not back well though.' She coughed as if to let Lydia know that she couldn't relax yet. Her breath smelt foul. 'Where's Joe?'

'He went to see if Mrs Shandu has anything to help your cough.'

'And to help my headache?'

'To help everything,' Lydia smiled.

'Will you tell me a story about Baba?'

'Of course,' said Lydia. 'I'll tell you about the time when he sat on the back of a donkey.'

'I like that one,' said Kesi.

'Well, Baba, he did some crazy things sometimes, and one day he decided to take a ride on a donkey. The donkey was happily munching at a clump of grass by the side of a path, when Baba hitched up his trousers and took a running jump on to its back. The donkey was so surprised that it took off, eee-awwing loudly as it galloped along the path and kicking its legs out every so often to try to unseat Baba. Now, Baba could be very stubborn, more stubborn than a donkey, and he wasn't going to let that donkey unseat him. So he hung on tight, arms stretched round the poor animal's neck, his legs squeezing its body. Your mama and Joe and I stood by the side of the path and howled with laughter. You've never seen such a funny sight. And then, all of sudden, the donkey stopped but Baba didn't. He flew over the top of its head.'

'And he landed in a muddy puddle, didn't he, Liddy?' giggled Kesi. 'I wish I'd seen him.' Then she added, sadly, 'I don't remember Baba, except for when he gave me a carry on his shoulders.'

'That's a good memory,' said Lydia, wishing that her own memories of their father were not tainted, particularly at that moment. 'Hang on tight to it, like Baba did to the donkey.'

Kesi giggled again, which set off a fit of coughing – hard, sharp explosions that left her heaving for breath. She sank down under the blanket and asked, in the smallest whisper, when Joe would be back. Lydia said he would be as quick as he could, but it was a long way to Mrs Shandu's homestead. Kesi closed her eyes and fell into another troubled sleep.

The wait for Joe to return seemed endless, but at last Lydia heard his footsteps outside and rushed to the door. By then, Kesi had coughed up more fetid green phlegm and her breathing was faster and more shallow than ever. She woke at the sound of Joe's voice and asked hoarsely if he had brought her anything.

'I've got you some funny drink that Mrs Shandu says will make your throat go warm,' said Joe.

He gave it to Lydia, who tipped a small amount into a cup and held it out for Kesi to drink. Kesi tried some and spat it out.

'Tastes yuck,' she moaned.

'Drink it, Kes, or you won't get better.'

Reluctantly Kesi did as she was told, then curled up in a ball without another word.

Joe took Lydia aside. 'Mrs Shandu says we must get her to hospital if she's worse in the morning,' he whispered. 'She says Kesi's too young to fight off a major infection on her own. And she's given us some money to help pay for any medicine. She's sorry it's not more, but she hasn't any more to spare.' He pulled a few coins from his pocket and handed them to Lydia.

Lydia took them and put them on the table. 'I hope we won't need to use them,' she said. 'Some people are so kind, Joe. I hope we can repay her one day. And thank you, Joe, just for being you. Mama would be so proud of you.'

Joe nodded. 'I think she'd be proud of all of us,' he said.

Chapter 20

Kesi was worse by the early hours of the morning, and tearful. She ached all over, she said, and her mouth was caked with a yellowy crust. It hurt her to breathe and she had no appetite, even though she hadn't eaten the day before. Lydia roused Joe.

'We need to get Kes to the hospital,' she said.

'How are we going to do that?' he groaned as he crawled out of bed. 'There won't be a bus for ages and we'll never be able to carry her.'

Lydia knew that wasn't an option. The hospital was more than two hours' walk away. 'Do you think you could go up to the road, Joe, and see if you can flag down a truck?'

Joe groaned again, but Lydia knew it was the struggle of waking up rather than a protest at what he was being asked to do. 'It's still dark outside,' he said.

'Take one of the lamps.'

Joe climbed into his clothes and dashed out of the rondavel. Lydia held a cup of water to Kesi's mouth. She couldn't drink, so Lydia dipped a finger into the water and dabbed it round her parched lips. Then she took a damp cloth and wiped her forehead. The sound of her sister's coughing filled her with anxiety. She tried not to think of her mother's warning words, but the longer she waited for Joe to return, the more they prised their way through her defences.

'Come on, Joe,' she urged. 'Please be quick.'

At last he appeared at the door. 'First there was nobody,' he said, 'and then three trucks drove straight past, and then one stopped.'

'Thank goodness,' cried Lydia. She jumped to her feet, lifted Kesi from the bed, turned and came face to face with Jabu. She was so shocked, she staggered backwards and had to be steadied by Joe.

'There was no one else,' he said.

'Not you,' she cried.

'I don't think you have a choice,' Jabu said, not mockingly but in a matter-of-fact voice.

'He said he'd drive us to the hospital, Liddy, and he doesn't want any money.'

Lydia glanced at the money she had put on the table and indicated that Joe should pick it up.

'Let me carry her,' Jabu said firmly. When Lydia hesitated, he added, 'I'm not going to harm her and I don't want anything in return.'

Lydia gave in. She had to take him at his word. There was no time to lose. 'Quickly, please go quickly,' she urged.

They hurried up the path and climbed into the truck, Joe in the middle next to Jabu, and Lydia by the window with Kesi huddled on her lap. For the first few kilometres or so, nobody spoke. The noise of the engine and Kesi's wheezing were the only sounds. Jabu lit a cigarette, but threw it away when it made her cough.

'She sounds bad,' he said. 'Has she been like that long?'

'Since yesterday morning,' Lydia replied.

'That quick, eh?' said Jabu. 'Must have been brewing it some time.'

Lydia nodded. Joe sat grim-faced, staring straight ahead.

'Lucky I stopped,' Jabu said.

Lydia nodded again and shifted uncomfortably.

'I was on my way from seeing my girlfriend. Don't tell your grandma, though. She wouldn't approve.'

Joe looked round at Lydia. Lydia bit her lip and focused on the road ahead.

'No, she's got other ideas for me. She likes to have her own way does your grandma.'

Lydia could feel Jabu staring across the cab at her. What sort of game was he playing now? Why couldn't he just drive and leave them alone? Kesi stirred and said she felt sick. Jabu lurched to a halt.

'Don't want that in my truck,' he grimaced.

He opened the door and helped Lydia down. She tried to concentrate on Kesi, who dropped to her knees and retched until there was nothing left to come out. Even Jabu looked concerned when they got back into the cab. He stopped talking and began to drive faster. Kesi sobbed into Lydia's lap, saying that she wanted her mama. Lydia saw that Joe looked petrified. She tried to hold his hand, but he pulled it away when he thought Jabu had noticed. Joe closed his eyes. For a while Lydia did the same.

It was much lighter outside when Jabu made them jump by turning on his radio. 'Nearly there now,' he said.

They stared out of the windows. The swathes of grassland randomly scattered with thatch-topped ron-davels had given way to rows of shabby wooden shacks with aluminium roofs. Stray dogs scavenged in and out of the gaps between the shacks, searching for scraps while the narrow streets were still quiet. A group of women stood by a solitary tap at the end of one row, while along another street traders were setting up tables stacked with vegetables, meats, machine parts and household goods. In one small shack, a man was having his hair cut. In the shack next door, a coffin-maker was already hard at work planing a plank of wood. None of this was a surprise to Lydia and Joe. They had travelled through shanty towns before, when their parents were alive. Passing through this one now made Lydia even more determined that she would never live in one, however hard their life became in the village.

When the road eventually opened up again, they saw a tall, grey building, surrounded by smaller out-buildings, with a crowd of people waiting outside.

'This is it,' said Jabu. 'We might have to push our way in. Looks like there's a bit of a queue.'

Lydia had been going to express their gratitude and suggest that he could leave them when they arrived, but as soon as she saw the crowd, she was relieved that he suggested he should carry Kesi inside.

'They'll shove you out of the way,' he said, 'but they won't argue with me.'

He took Kesi from her arms. Kesi was so weak that she didn't protest. She coughed pathetically. Lydia told her to be brave and that she would be better very soon. Joe followed behind, shoulders hunched up, face tense.

As soon as Jabu reached the edge of the crowd, he began to push through it. The crowd reacted angrily.

'Where do you think you're going?' one man shouted. 'Some of us have been waiting here for hours.'

'You can't just push in,' cried another.

'Can't you see this child is dying?' demanded Jabu. 'Do you want her death on your hands?'

When she heard this, Lydia wanted to cry out. She kept her head down though, afraid that someone might challenge her as well. She gripped Joe's arm so that he wouldn't be separated from them, and moved forward with him. The crowd allowed them through, some of them still complaining. However, a guard stationed at the hospital doors barred their entrance.

'The hospital's full,' he said. 'They can't take anyone else.'

'They'll take this child,' said Jabu, 'even if I have to knock you down to get in there.'

'Violence won't get you anywhere, except jail,' the guard sniffed. 'What's the matter with her then?'

'Am I the doctor? While you're standing there asking dumb questions, she could die. Now are you going to let me in, or are you going to stand there and watch as she breathes her last breath?'

'You'll get me sacked,' the guard muttered, but he beckoned them forward. 'Go through quickly, before you cause a riot.'

He opened the doors so that they could just about squeeze through, then banged them shut again as the crowd pressed towards them. Once inside, they hurried along a dimly lit corridor, until a nurse stopped them and asked what they thought they were doing. This time it was Lydia who spoke.

'It's my sister,' she said. 'She's ill, really ill. Please help her.'

The nurse took one look at Kesi and told Jabu to put her down on a table that served as a bed.

'Are you the father?' she asked him, as she took Kesi's temperature.

'No!' he snorted. 'Not me, ma'am. I'm just the driver.'

'Then I must ask you to leave. We only allow relatives in here.'

Jabu put up his hands in surrender. 'Don't shoot,' he said. 'I get the message.'

He saluted Lydia and Joe, then turning serious, he said, 'I hope little sister will be all right.'

Lydia nodded. 'Thank you,' she said. 'Thank you for your help.'

'That's what friends are for, isn't it?' he grinned.

Chapter 21

For three days Kesi lay critically ill. Lydia and Joe could only sit and watch as doctors and nurses came and went. There were several crises when it seeemed as if Kesi's frail body would succumb to the infection that raged within her – pneumonia with complications, one of the doctors told them.

'We're running tests,' he said, 'and we'll know more when we have the results. But your sister is very ill. Is there anyone else who should know?'

Lydia shook her head. 'My parents both died. There's nobody. You won't let Kesi die, will you? I promised Mama I'd look after her.'

The doctor put a hand on her shoulder. 'We're doing our best,' he said. 'The next twenty-four hours will tell.'

Kesi developed a fever and her temperature soared. Lydia and Joe were already exhausted from lack of sleep and little to eat. The third night seemed to go on for ever. They sat in the bleak corridor, listening to the moans and groans of the other patients, waiting for some word that would give them hope. They saw nurses shaking their heads and feared the worst, but were told that their sister was a little fighter. By the early hours of the morning, unable to keep their eyes open any longer, they had stretched out on the floor, wrapped themselves round each other and fallen into an uneasy sleep.

It seemed only seconds later, though the nurse assured them that it was the middle of the morning, when she gently shook them awake.

They struggled unsteadily to their feet to hear her say, 'Your little sister is asking for you.'

Lydia searched the nurse's face for some sort of explanation.

The nurse smiled. 'She's made it through,' she said. 'She's very weak, but she's out of danger. You got her here in time.'

Lydia was so overwhelmed with relief that she burst into tears. Joe put his arm round her.

'You're supposed to be happy, Liddy, not cry,' he said.

'I am happy,' she spluttered. 'Come on, let's go and see her.'

They followed the nurse to Kesi's bedside. Lydia was disturbed by how thin her sister had become in such a short time, and once again the doubts came about what lay behind her illness. She had a tube sticking up her nose, a drip by the side of her bed and was propped up slightly on a grubby pillow. Her eyes were closed.

'She looks awful, Liddy,' whispered Joe.

Lydia nodded and took Kesi's hand. Her eyes opened straight away and she tried to sit up.

'Don't tire yourself, Kes,' said Lydia.

'Can't I go home now?' she murmured.

'Not until you're a bit stronger.'

'I'm hungry.'

'That's good,' said Lydia. 'It means you're getting better.'

'I don't like this thing up my nose. Can I take it out now?'

'Not until the doctor says.'

'People snore in here. Big loud snores like pigs do.' Kesi giggled.

'Shhh!' smiled Lydia. 'You'll have us thrown out.'

The doctor who had spoken to Lydia previously came over and checked Kesi's notes. 'She's doing well,' he nodded approvingly. 'Can I have a word, in private?'

Lydia wanted Joe to go with her, but she didn't like to leave Kesi on her own. She followed the doctor, a knot of dread tying itself up inside her. He showed her into a small office and indicated that she should sit down. She perched on the edge of the chair.

'Your sister has been extremely ill,' he said. 'Luckily, she has a very strong immune system and so her body has fought back, though it will be several months before she is fully recovered.'

Lydia bit her lip, waiting for him to tell her the worst.

'What I am saying here is that if her immune system had been compromised, she might not have been able to fight back. The tests are negative, Lydia. Kesi doesn't have AIDS.'

Lydia's mouth dropped open and her eyes widened. The beginnings of a smile tugged at her lips. 'Are you sure?' she breathed.

'As sure as I can be,' he smiled.

'I've got to tell Joe!' Lydia scrambled to her feet and rushed out of the door. She was so overwhelmed with joy that she had to share it with him right there and then. She tore along the corridor. When she reached the ward, she called out to him. He stood up to see what the matter was.

'She's all right, Joe,' she said, heading towards him. 'I mean, she's really, really all right.'

She watched Joe's tense face relax into the biggest smile she had seen for a very long time. They hugged each other, laughing and crying so much that one of the other patients called out, 'Someone's happy!'

'Yes,' grinned Lydia. 'We're happy. Very happy.'

Chapter 22

Two days later, they were able to take Kesi home.

'Remember,' said the nurse, 'she is still a very sick little girl and if we had the beds we would keep her here longer. You must make sure she takes her medicine every day, and she must rest.'

A shock of cold air greeted them as they stepped outside the hospital doors and pushed through the waiting crowd. They took a deep draught of it to clear their lungs of the stale, stifling air they had been breathing over the past five days. Kesi shivered and pulled Lydia and Joe closer.

'Let's hope the bus comes soon,' said Joe. 'It's too cold for Kes to be out here for long.'

'Your wish has been answered,' smiled Lydia when a bus appeared on the horizon.

They scrambled on board, Lydia handing the driver

the last of the money Mrs Shandu had given her. They squeezed in amongst the other passengers, one of whom made room for Kesi to sit down. As the bus rumbled along the rutted road, Lydia tried to hang on to the feelings of happiness that had continued to engulf her as Kesi grew stronger and stronger. She wanted to believe that they had turned a corner, that life was going to become easier. Kesi didn't have AIDS. That was a huge weight of worry off her mind. They had friends in Mrs Shandu and Mandisa – without Mrs Shandu's kindness they wouldn't have been able to pay for Kesi's treatment and they would be walking home now.

Even Jabu had been kind to them. She wondered why and whether it was something she should be concerned about. Would he expect to be repaid? She didn't trust him, couldn't trust him, but she wanted to think that perhaps he had softened in the face of Kesi's illness. And hadn't he said that he had a girl-friend? It was all so confusing.

Lydia pushed away thoughts of her grandmother. They weren't for now. Grandma Motsie must have known about Kesi's illness – Jabu surely would have told her – but she hadn't been to visit and hadn't offered her support. She had lost the power, in those hours of sheer joy, to do them any harm, whatever might happen later. Lydia squeezed Kesi's shoulder and smiled at Joe. She couldn't wait to get home and sleep in her own bed. She willed the journey to be over. The bus stopped so many times to let passengers on and off, Lydia almost felt the driver was doing it on purpose, just to make her wait even longer.

At last, she saw the familiar sprawl of the village open out in front of her. Familiar, yet somehow different. The gently rolling slopes with their patchwork of rondavels looked fresher, brighter.

'We're nearly there, Kes,' she whispered.

Kesi tried to stand up to see, but her legs gave way with the effort of peering through the tangle of bodies that surrounded her.

Lydia was surprised at how excited she felt about going home, but she was anxious too. The thoughts she had banished came back to assault her. If Jabu had told Grandma Motsie about their prolonged absence, would their home still be empty when they returned? Would their grandmother have seized the opportunity to snatch it from them?

The bus stopped. They clambered off and walked slowly along the road, fighting against a sniping wind. It was still some distance to their homestead and Kesi could not be hurried. With every step, Lydia's anxiety grew, while Joe chattered to her happily about going back to school.

'What's up, Liddy?' he asked. 'You don't seem very happy suddenly.'

Lydia shook her head. 'It's nothing, Joe. I'm just a bit tired.'

They came to the path that led down to the rondavel. Lydia hesitated at the top. Joe broke into a run and flew down the path, making engine noises. Kesi giggled and tried to copy him, until Lydia stopped her. Joe turned through the gap in the hedge. Lydia listened for some cry, some shout that would tell her the worst.

It didn't come. Joe's face poked round the edge of the hedge. 'Hurry up, Liddy,' he called. 'You should see the garden. The seedlings are nearly double the size.'

'Is our home all right?' she called back.

'It hasn't gone anywhere,' he chuckled.

Lydia ran towards him, aiming a playful swipe at his head as she rounded the hedge. She was struck by how green the garden looked. And the rondavel was sitting there patiently waiting for them.

'Let's get you inside, Kes,' she said.

'At least I won't have to listen to big snores tonight,' she pouted.

'Little rumbles from Joe, that's all,' Lydia grinned.

'I won't fetch the water if you're rude about me,' he warned, taking the jug and heading straight off.

As soon as they were indoors, Lydia felt their home fold itself round them like a cosy cocoon. She tucked Kesi up in bed, and even before Joe had returned her sister was sound asleep, wheezing gently, her frizz of hair spiralling across the pillow, lips quivering. Lydia stared at her and understood what it must feel like to be a mother gazing down at her child. If only their mother could be there now. If only she had lived long enough to know that Kesi was safe.

Later that day, Mandisa arrived with a bag of rice and vegetables.

'I've come here every day to see if you were back,' she said. 'We've been so worried about you. Grandma wanted you to have these. It's not much, but it will help a bit.'

Lydia gave her friend a hug. 'Thank you so much. You're all so kind.'

'You'll never believe what's happening at school.

There's a group of travelling actors coming to do a play and they're going to do some work with us as well. Wouldn't you just love to act?'

Where did it come from, that talent for wrapping your-self up in somebody else's identity and presenting it as your own?

Lydia nodded. 'I'd like to be a nurse as well,' she said, 'especially after seeing what they did for Kes.'

'How will you do that if you don't come back to school? You should try to come back, Lydia. I miss having you there.'

'I miss being there. Maybe when Kes is better.'

'I'll get Grandma to nag you. Everybody gives in when Grandma nags!'

It was all so much easier for her friend, Lydia thought, wistfully but without any resentment.

'I wish we had a grandmother like yours,' she said.

Chapter 23

Two days after they had returned home, Lydia was sweeping the yard when Jabu appeared through the hedge. She stopped what she was doing and braced herself.

'Need any help?' he asked. He took a long drag of a cigarette, threw down the butt and ground it into the earth with the heel of his boot.

She shook her head. 'No. Thank you.'

'How's the little girl?'

'She's doing well. She's sleeping. Thank you for what you did for us.'

'It was nothing,' he said.

If that was why he had come, to see how Kesi was, Lydia wished he would go now. She stood there awkwardly while he looked round the garden.

'Your vegetables are looking healthy,' he said. 'I'm impressed. You're more than just a pretty face.'

Lydia scowled. He was starting on her again.

'Oh dear. I've just gone and spoilt it,' he mocked. She dropped the broom and turned to go indoors.

'Wait,' he said. 'I've got something for you.'

She hesitated, not wanting to look round in case it was a trick.

'Relax, Lydia. I told you, I've got a girlfriend. And she comes with a nice big farm.'

She swung round, ready to tell him to go away and leave her alone, when he held something out to her.

'Take it,' he said.

It was a wad of papers.

'Your grandma told me she didn't need my services any more, and since she decided not to pay me what I was owed, I helped myself to something rather valuable – at least to her. And, I reckon, to you.'

The land documents.

Lydia stared at them, then looked at Jabu, expecting there to be some catch.

'Take them,' he said again. He pushed them into her hands. 'You'd better look after them this time, though I don't think your grandma will have expected me to give them back to you.'

'Why?' Lydia asked. 'Why are you doing this for us?'

'Can't resist a pretty face, I suppose,' he grinned. 'You're a feisty one, you are, Lydia. Good luck to you all. You won't see me again.'

He touched a finger to his forehead and strode away.

Lydia stood for a moment, staring at the gap through the hedge, then she ran inside, clutching the land documents to her chest. She was so happy she almost forgot that Kesi was lying there.

'Who was outside?' her sister asked.

'Jabu came to see how you are.'

'You don't like Jabu.'

'Not much, but he helped us when you had to go to the hospital.'

'I don't remember.'

Lydia sat down on the bed next to Kesi and gave her an enormous hug.

'Everything's going to be all right, Kes. I just know it. You're going to get better, and the garden's growing, and you and Joe can keep going to school, and we've got friends.'

'What about Grandma?'

'Grandma will be a very lonely old lady without her family. She can't harm us any more, Kes. We're too strong for her.'

'Will we be able to eat?'

'Are you hungry?'

Kesi nodded.

'We'll always struggle to find enough to eat,' said Lydia. 'But today, I'll make you a feast.'

Before she began to cook, Lydia lifted Kesi on to a chair, stripped the bed and turned the mattress over. Much to Kesi's amazement, she took a knife and made a large cut through the outer material.

'Why are you cutting the bed up, Liddy?'

'I want to hide something in it so that nobody can find it. It'll be our secret hiding place.'

When the slit was long enough, Lydia pushed the land documents through it and sewed it back up. 'There,' she said. 'Nobody will ever find them there.'

'What if I wee the bed?' asked Kesi.

'You won't,' said Lydia. 'You haven't done that for ages.'

She turned the mattress over again, put it back on the bedframe and settled Kesi down, just as Joe came home.

'Guess who's been picked as captain of the football team,' he said, nose in the air, grinning broadly.

'Let me think,' said Lydia. 'I guess Mbeke.'

'No, silly,' chuckled Kesi. 'Joe means *he's* been picked.'

'Does he? Have you, Joe?'

'First match tomorrow,' he said loftily.

'That's fantastic, Joe. Well done. That's even more reason for us to have a feast tonight.'

'What's the other reason?' Joe asked.

'Grandma's going to be lonely without us and she can't harm us and we've got a secret hiding place,' piped up Kesi, pointing under the mattress and putting a finger across her lips.

'I stitched the documents that prove this homestead belongs to us into the mattress to keep them safe,' explained Lydia.

'Good idea,' said Joe. 'We don't want anyone stealing them. Especially Grandma.'

'We're too strong for Grandma,' said Kesi.

That evening was the best they had had as a family of three. While Lydia cooked, Joe read to Kesi. After they had eaten and were groaning about the fullness of their bellies, they played stones, giggling uncontrollably every time a stone or their tiny rubber ball fell off the table and rolled under the bed. When Kesi fell asleep, Lydia helped Joe with his maths and was delighted to discover there was the slightest sign that he was beginning to understand it.

'I was trying to think what's changed, Liddy,' he whispered as they lay in bed that night. 'I mean, not much has changed really, but we're much happier, aren't we?'

'We know that Kes hasn't got AIDS,' said Lydia.

'Yes, but we believed that before.'

'Believing and knowing aren't the same. Knowing has taken the doubt and the worry away.'

'So, what else?' said Joe. 'We'll still be hungry most of the time and we've still got a grandma who hates us.'

'We'll still be hungry, but we've taken control of our larder, and we'll still have to fetch water and do chores, but you're safely back at school. Grandma can't take that from you. She can't take anything from us unless we let her.'

'Just let her try,' said Joe.

'And you're football captain. That's a good enough reason on its own to be happy.'

Joe nodded and closed his eyes.

'There's one more thing,' whispered Lydia to herself. She slipped quietly out of bed and looked out of the window. The garden was bathed in light. The sky was cloudless and the moon was full.

You will never be alone, Lydia. I will always be there for you. Find your strength from me. Be that person we talked about who can climb the tallest tree and touch the moon.

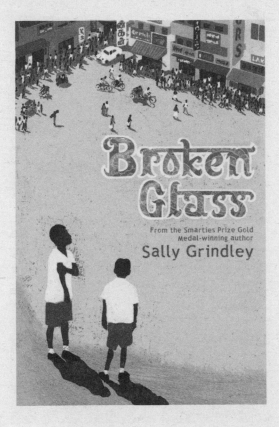

'Deserving Smarties Gold Award winner.
A powerful story'
The Sunday Times